CRISIS at Pemberton Dike

CRISIS at Pemberton Dike

Rachel Sherwood Roberts

HERALD PRESS
Scottdale, Pennsylvania
Kitchener, Ontario
1984

Library of Congress Cataloging in Publication Data

Roberts, Rachel Sherwood, 1940-
    Crisis at Pemberton Dike.

    Summary: Fifteen-year-old Carol is more interested in her school and
family activities than a spring flood but, as the rising waters of the three
rivers near her town threaten to overflow, she joines the many volunteers
helping to build and strengthen the levees and dikes needed to prevent
disaster.
    [1. Floods—Fiction.   2. Community life—Fiction]
I. Title.
PZ7.R54426Cr   1984   [Fic]   83-18664
ISBN 0-8361-3350-1 (pbk.)

.

CRISIS AT PEMBERTON DIKE
Copyright © 1984 by Herald Press, Scottdale, Pa. 15683
    Published simultaneously in Canada by Herald Press,
    Kitchener, Ont. N2G 4M5
Library of Congress Catalog Card Number: 83-18664
International Standard Book Number: 0-8361-3350-1
Printed in the United States of America
Designed by Alice B. Shetler

84 85 86 87 88 89 10 9 8 7 6 5 4 3 2 1

For my family,
   and all who treasure the specialness of family—

For my brave, caring, and accomplished sisters and brothers,
   especially Elza, sister of my childhood—

For victims of floods—
   and all who, in spite of danger and dreariness,
   sandbag, give time, food, money, medical care,
   housing, and help during clean up, and

For those who wish they could . . . .

Author's Note

Pemberton Dike is fiction based on the facts of the 1982 flood in northeast Indiana. Some details and names have been changed for the sake of the story (I have combined Pemberton Road Dike and Sherman Boulevard events), but the theme is indisputable. Today's young people are courageous and caring. They are ordinary citizens who represent the best qualities of working together to achieve the common good. They are our heroes.

CRISIS at Pemberton Dike

AT FIRST she didn't think about danger. In fact, it never crossed her mind. Carol was tired of hard, crusty, icy weather and wondered if school would again be canceled. Turning over sleepily, she reached toward her bedside table for the earphone to her portable radio. She didn't want to wake Nina, her nine-year-old sister, so she tried not to rattle the papers and magazines stacked by her clock. It was 5:00 a.m.! Of all the crazy times to wake up, she thought, yet, since she had, she might as well find out about school.

The announcers on WOWO's "Little Red Barn" program would already be visiting, discussing the roads and weather, and they would announce the school closings. If canceled, she'd be able to sleep another couple of hours or so and not worry about rushing to get ready for school. And, she'd have the weekend to complete her essay report, which Mr. Fowler expected to be on his desk today.

Her report was okay, she guessed, but if she had just one

more day, she'd be able to get it typed and that might really make a good impression. Maybe, just maybe, she'd be able to get an "A." Janice would positively die, but then, if Janice didn't stop her lofty way of snipping about grades, something was going to happen.

"I see you did okay on your test, getting a 'B+' and all," Janice had said Wednesday, casually letting her own paper fall on the table to display a neat little "A" in the upper right hand corner.

Rats! Carol had seethed. Just when had Janice started this self-imposed campaign to make her feel envious? Or was it something else? Carol didn't quite know, but she did know Janice was becoming more and more detestable.

The announcers were discussing fertilizers, special seed blends, and the weather. No school cancellations today. Carol groaned. Like it or not, the morning routine would soon start. Snow, snow, snow. It had been so beautiful when it first came down in December. Christmas had been as pretty as a postcard scene. But, after such a nice mild start, January hit the Midwest like a furious demon, bringing record snows, fierce howling winds, and cold freezing ice storms. All through February and March, the weather played havoc piling up huge drifts and mounds of slick ice and snow. And schools had been canceled day after day after day. Winter made a mockery of school schedules and family activities. Business was at a standstill. People were bone tired. Here it was almost St. Patrick's Day, usually a time her dad talked about planting early peas, and outside snow was four feet deep where the garden was supposed to be. Cars inched along deep narrow corridors, red ribbons tied to their antennas so oncoming traffic would be able to see past and around corners. It was strange, Carol thought. She'd never seen anything like this in all her 15 years!

Suddenly Carol roused from her dozing. Bob Sievers was talking about the weather again. She listened. "And there could be a danger of some flooding, especially if this snow begins to melt rapidly," another announcer said, "but for today, it will be sunny with a touch of spring, which goodness knows," he added in a relieved voice, "we certainly can use."

Oh, well, Carol thought, *I can still grab at least an hour or so more sleep before getting up.* She flicked off the radio, laid the earphone down, and snuggled under her quilt. *I'll just turn in my report the way it is,* she thought. *It's really not bad, even if it isn't the best I can do. Flooding? There could be no flooding. No way,* Carol mused. *It would take weeks for all that snow to melt. Bet I'll be able to find little piles of snow around the roots of trees or by the woodpile as late as June,* she thought.

A few hours later, Carol was happy to see the sky clear and blue. She hurried to wake Nina.

"Get up, you'll be late for school if you don't hurry. Besides, mom's already been in once to wake you. Hurry up. I'm not going to wait for a slowpoke." Carol pulled the covers back from Nina, who lay curled like a rose petal in the middle of her bed.

"Come on, Nina. Get up!" she said crossly, grabbing her brown tweed skirt and blue sweater from the closet. She'd get to the bathroom first, and Nina could fuss if she wanted. Would serve her right too!

"Mom," Carol said happily, bounding down the steps, "spring will come. Look at that sunshine! Remember how you've hated all these cloudy days! Here, I'll pour the orange juice. And mom, Nina's not half ready."

"Oh, you girls," her mother answered. "Every morning the same fuss. It isn't necessary, you know, to quarrel just

11

because you get up first. Here's the bread for your toast. Dad's coming in a minute."

"Hi, dad," Carol smiled at her father.

"Why so happy this morning?" he asked.

"The sun. I just love the sun. It seems like a month since we've seen the sun. I think spring is really coming."

Walt Norton smiled at his daughter. "You've always been our little barometer. If it is sunny, you're sunny. If it's cloudy, well, you're kind of like that."

"You're just teasing," Carol said and laughed. "You know how we need a change in the weather. I'll admit, though, I did enjoy all those snow days, but I knew it wouldn't last."

"Yes, you'll have to start going to school again whether you like it or not," her dad said.

"Nina, hurry up," her mother called.

"Coming."

"Well, come on so we can get started! I'm starving," Carol added.

"Mom, Carol is yelling at me again!"

"Girls, come on now. Settle down. Let's have a good breakfast." It was plain to see her dad was not going to put up with a squabble of any kind this morning.

"Walt, the groundhog is out."

"The what?" Carol's dad asked.

"The old groundhog, remember?" Millie said. "Early this morning when I came down to fix breakfast, I saw that fat thing waddling out from right under our deck."

"You mean he's here again this year?" the girls chimed.

"There he is now! Look, he's got leaves in his mouth."

"Where did he get leaves this time of year, mom?"

"From way back under the deck, I guess, Nina. There he goes. Look how he's leaving a muddy reddish brown trail in the snow."

"That seems funny. I haven't seen any dirt in ages," Carol said.

"Mom, do you think he's getting ready to make a nest?" Nina asked.

"Maybe, if he's a she," Carol answered.

The Nortons laughed and craned their necks to see more from the sliding glass door, but the groundhog scurried into his hole.

"Well, Millie," Walt Norton said, grinning at his wife, "we can honestly say winter's back is broken, can't we?"

In spite of the mounds and mounds of snow, in spite of all the trees and shrubs that looked dry and brittle, the Nortons knew they could live with whatever new ice storms or snow might come. The old groundhog showed them what nature knew. In the dark cracks and corners of the earth, deep under blankets of snow and ice, little urges and rushes were turning, mysteriously answering primitive, inexplicable calls, moving with the axis of the world, responding to God's creative plan. Spring would indeed come. The groundhog announced it.

Carol looked at her watch. "Have to go. We've got to be in our desks by 8:30. Come on, Nina. Don't dawdle! I'm not going to wait for you today, and I won't be late because of you!"

"Mother, Carol's making me mad, and where's my scarf and mittens?"

"Right where you left them yesterday. Hurry up, Nina. Carol may just have a point about your being slow this morning."

"Don't forget, girls, watch for traffic. Those drifts are so high, you can't see when a car comes along. With that ice storm we had two days ago, they don't have much traction either. Try to walk up on the mounds away from the cars."

13

"Dad, you tell us that every day," Nina said. "Besides, there's just no place to walk but straight down the middle of the road."

"You can at least see the cars that way," Carol said, buttoning her coat. "Besides, only one car can go through at a time."

"Good-bye, girls." Millie set down her coffee cup. "If you need anything today, I'll be home. I can't go anywhere in weather like this. I'm glad you don't have far to walk."

"Wish you'd drive us, mom," Nina said.

"Go on now. A little walk two blocks or so won't do anything but give you beautiful skin," Millie Norton said. "It'll wake you up too!"

"Besides, I'm walking also," Walt Norton added. "It'll keep your old pop young."

"Oh, dad," Nina called back, her words forming a cloud of vapor in the air. "You're young to me anyway."

The girls waved, their red mittens making bright circles against the background.

"Millie, it's pretty out there, don't you think?"

"It's beautiful, but I really hate it when it all starts to melt. It gets so messy and gray."

"And slushy," Walt said.

"I don't like the girls walking when there's so much slush. Every car that comes along just spews and sprays the stuff all over everything."

Millie sighed. "They're growing up too fast, Walt. Do we tell them enough how special and loved they are?"

Walt grinned. "At least 365 times a year, I'd guess. Well, I'd better get going too. You going to tell me I'm special?"

Millie laughed. "You know you are, silly." She smiled at her husband and began clearing the table.

At the corner of First and Green Briar, Carol caught the

bus for Auburn High School. She waved good-bye to Nina, who only had one more block to walk before reaching Auburn Elementary.

"See you," Carol said, climbing into the bus. Sitting down next to Reba Breenan, Carol asked, "Got your report for Mr. Fowler?"

"Yeah, I finished it just in the nick of time."

"I was hoping for a snow day again today. Look at that bright sunshine," Carol said. "Guess we've had our share of snow days. Actually, to tell you the truth, I sort of feel behind in several of my classes."

"Yeah, like those math problems we're supposed to know how to do," Reba said, clutching her books. "Look how steamy it gets in here."

"I hate buses," Carol said. "I can't wait until I can drive."

"Or be driven to school each day like Mary Tree," Reba said.

"Must be nice."

"I'll bet Mary Tree's got a thousand dollars in the bank just to spend," Reba added.

"I heard she plans to go to some fancy place this summer," Carol said.

"Yeah, she can't stick around and do dumb things like the rest of us. It sure must be nice."

"Hey, look at this, Reba." Carol reached in her book bag for her report. "Bet you thought I'd be late with this, huh? I wanted mom to type it so it would look sharp, but she wouldn't."

"Why did you want it typed?"

"Well, then I'd show it to Janice, and maybe, just maybe, her's wouldn't be."

"You two still doing that sort of thing?" Reba asked.

"Well, you know how she likes to brag."

"You aren't so bad," Reba teased. "You're one of the best, and you know it."

"Reba, cut that out. You'd say that even if you knew I was awful. It isn't fair."

"But you aren't awful," Reba said. "You know that."

"I'm not good all the time either."

"You're better than a lot of people, Carol, and you've got tons of friends. Even Dick Moore thinks you're sharp, and he's the best looking guy in our class."

"Dick Moore is a jerk, Reba. When you gonna see through all his talk?" Carol was annoyed. Couldn't Reba see beyond her nose? She decided not to show Reba her report. She put it back. Shifting in her seat, she stared out at the snow.

Reba said nothing. As the bus came to a stop, students scrambled to get out. Carol said, "Bye, Reba. Have a good time in gym class. I'll see you in English."

"Yeah, see ya," Reba answered lamely.

"Hey, good-looking," Dick Moore said casually to Reba as she hurried up the steps, but he seemed to be looking at Carol. The frosty air hit Carol in the face and made her shiver. She pulled her scarf closer, and said, "When did it get so cold?"

"It's been cold all winter," Dick laughed. "Where've you been?"

"Winter's back is broken," Carol said. "We saw the old groundhog this morning during breakfast. He was scurrying around, and you never saw such a fat thing!"

"Well, that's a sure sign, but all he'll find behind your house is snow and ice, five feet deep."

"Yeah, he could build an igloo."

"You know something, Carol," Dick said, "it could be a

disaster if all this snow melted fast."

"I won't think about that. It'll never happen. We'll be seeing snow next June. You can bet on it!" Carol chuckled. "I'm sick of winter, aren't you?"

"You can say that again," Dick answered. "At first it was fun with everything being canceled. I've never seen anything like this, though. It's really strange."

The door made a whooshing noise behind them as it closed. They hurried to get to their homerooms. "Do you have your report ready for Mr. Fowler?"

"Yeah, he won't have to crawl all over me with sarcasm about being late," Carol laughed. "I'll just turn it in and forget it. You got yours?"

"Oh, sure," Dick said. "Copied it right out of the encyclopedia, no problem. Just changed a few sentences around here and there. Can you imagine having a topic on the common mosquito?"

"Well, what about mine? I had to look up and report about the planet Jupiter."

"Do you know, Carol," Mary Tree chimed in, "I heard somebody on television talking about some scary kind of thing that's going to happen. It's called the Jupiter Concept. All about the planets lining up and the world being pulled by the gravity. We're supposed to have terrible earthquakes and floods and all sorts of things. Some people think the end of the world is going to come."

"Oh, cut that out, Mary. You're trying to be dramatic. Couldn't be," Dick scoffed.

"Yeah, Mary," Carol added. "You can go watch the world come to an end if you want to, but I've got to get to class."

Dumbsville! How could those people be so gullible? Was she the only sensible person around? She viewed things much more reasonably. Carol wondered why. Maybe it was because her family talked so much. Before anything came up at school, the Norton family probably had discussed it during one of their meals. The Jupiter Concept? She pulled out her math book. We're much more likely to have a silly flood. The world coming to an end? It did make a person wonder, though. Maybe all those air currents were getting zoomed out of whack with all the stuff the government had put into orbit and outer space. Maybe that's why we've had such an awful winter. Records broken all over the place. Even her dad said he couldn't remember a winter like this one. *It's sure something to think about,* Carol mused.

She wouldn't be able to come back to her locker before English class so she'd better take her report with her. She pulled out her green folder. Opening it she was pleased with the way the first page looked. She liked the way she'd spaced her title, "The Mighty Planet Jupiter" by Carol Lee Norton.

Turning to the second page, Carol gasped. "Oh, no!" She felt herself stiffen with anger and defeat. Her eyes stung. "Wait till I get my hands on Nina!" she muttered. "I'm ruined!"

Chapter 2

"MOTHER, I hate Nina. I can't take her anymore. I won't have her messing up my stuff. How would you feel if your report was ruined? Just because of some grimy nine-year-old sister who is mean and nasty and . . . ."

"Just a minute, Carol," her mother ordered. "What are you talking about and what do you mean saying those things about your sister? You will *not* talk about your sister that way, and you will *not* use that word 'hate!' "

"Mother," Carol wailed. "She ruined my report. She does things on purpose. She spilled her orange juice last night on my desk and she said it didn't get on anything. Well, you should have seen my report. It was smeared, messy, and all wrinkled where she'd tried to mop up the juice with her towel."

"Oh, no. On your English report?"

"Yes, the one I worked on so hard. The one I wanted you to type and you wouldn't. Mother, I can't stand Nina. I'm fifteen years old, and I don't have anything I can call my own. Everything I have, she wants. Everything I do, she wants to do. I need some privacy. It isn't fair," Carol stormed.

"Now sit here and calm down. What did you do? How did you handle it? What did Mr. Fowler say?" Her mother felt sorry for Carol, but she wouldn't put up with her temper.

"Oh, mother, I turned it in anyway. But how would you have felt? I'm so mad."

"I know, I know," her mother said. "It must have been awful. You know Nina wouldn't do that on purpose. You know that. Have you talked to her?"

"I don't want to talk to her. I don't even want to see her face. She's coming home around four o'clock because of some class thing of hers. But she better not come home at all!"

"Carol, stop that talk right now! Get yourself under control, young lady! I know you're disappointed, but you're also angry, and you're not thinking straight. What if you'd spilled something on Nina's work?"

"Would serve her right!"

"Oh, no, no, Carol. That isn't right. You know about forgiveness. I know you feel upset. Come on, tell me about it. What did Mr. Fowler say?"

"He laughed."

"He laughed?"

"Yes, he laughed. He said it reminded him about one time when he had to turn in a college paper, and he'd stayed up all night to work on it. The next morning before going to class, he stopped by the college coffee shop to have breakfast, and the waitress spilled coffee all over his paper."

"Well, honey. He did understand then."

"I guess so, but I really wanted that paper to look sharp. You know how Janice is always gloating about her grades. She's such a pain. I guess I wanted, just once, to get a better grade than she did."

"Well, Mr. Fowler could tell you were disappointed. I'm glad he was understanding. Some teachers can be terrible about things like that. I remember a teacher I once had who was a tyrant."

"Yeah, like Mrs. Martin. If this had happened in her class, she would have raved and raved. I'd hate to have her for English."

Mrs. Norton patted Carol on the arm. "You'll feel better soon. Thank goodness, Mr. Fowler was understanding. Don't be too hard on Nina. It was an accident, you know."

"She's always having some kind of accident, mom. I don't think it's fair. I really need a place of my own."

"We'll think about that. Maybe you do. Carol, your room is so large and runs the entire length of the upstairs on that side of the house. Maybe it could be partitioned or something."

"Please, mother. I can't take this much longer. Last week she had all her posters and crayons spread on the worktable, and she got paint on my best blouse."

"Your light blue one?"

"Yes, I'm tired of her. She's always doing something messy."

"I'll think about it, Carol. I'll talk to your dad. But I don't promise a thing. By the way, you've got time to practice your piano before Nina gets home. Why not do it now?"

"Because I'm going to call Alice Lewiston. She wanted me to call her at four. I'll do the piano later."

"Well, you've got to get it done."

"I'm hungry, mom. Anything in the cookie can?"

"I don't know. Your father came home for lunch and may have swiped a few. We'll be eating soon, though. Have an apple or some cheese instead."

While her mother rummaged around in the pantry for something, Carol walked to the back window and looked out over the flood plain. The sun had melted the snow just enough for a long line to form in the middle of the valley. It looked like a thin gray thread lying in the snow. *That line will widen by tomorrow, if we're lucky enough to have another sunny day,* Carol thought. It seemed all the days in March had been dreary and cloudy, usually with a biting raw wind that whipped around making tree limbs snap rakishly back and forth. She leaned her forehead against the sliding patio door. "I wish I were a million miles away from this place," she whispered to herself. She heard the phone ring and heard her mother answer.

Carol knew the old routine. Always the same. Her dad calling to say he'd be home in about an hour. Honestly, whatever could he find to say to her mother? They talked all the time. They had had lunch together. Sometimes he'd call during the day to talk. And at night, there was always conversation again. As she thought about her parents, she realized how good it would be to have someone she could talk with. Reba was such a louse, always telling her things she wanted to hear. Dick Moore wasn't too sharp either. Mary Tree seemed too taken with herself. Nobody really understands me, she thought. Nobody except maybe mother. She tries, at least. But she doesn't really understand. And Nina? Oh, no! Just thinking about her made Carol feel confused. *Is it hate,* she wondered? *I do hate her, yet I would die if anything happened to her. Love-hate. Maybe that was it. What a deal! She should have told me about messing up my report!* Carol felt tired, angry, and depressed. *I've been angry a lot lately,* she thought. *People irritate me. They just don't seem to know much about anything. I don't either, but somehow it's different. I don't try to play their "I-know-it-all" game, or do I?* She stared out at the flood plain, the watershed area that formed a valley between the bluff on which their house was situated and Cedar Creek running along the back edge of their property. On the bluff just below the deck, the old groundhog had his cave. The flood plain often looked like an overgrown weedy riverbed and beyond it, grew a thin stand of trees. During the winter, the Nortons could see lights from houses beyond the creek. But during the summer, the underbrush and trees formed a dense backdrop of green making the Norton place seem as isolated as if it were country. By contrast, in their front yard, however, the street circled giving the four neighboring houses graceful front lawns. Carol looked down at the valley. Shadows stretched across the snow and moved up the bluff where the deck of her house extended. White, icy, cold snow. Would it ever go away? Even Nina's swing set stood resolutely amid all the snow, the swings buried hard in the drifts. Carol hoped for another sunny day. It had been such a nice change.

"Carol?" Nina called. "Carol?"

"What?"

"Carol, I'm sorry about your report." Nina came in the family room dumping her backpack on the green chair. "Mom told me you were mad. I'm sorry. It *was* an accident."

"Some accident. You should have told me." Carol turned, squared her shoulders, and glared at Nina.

"I didn't do it on purpose, honestly."

"Why didn't you tell me? That way at least I could have copied the page over."

"I don't know, Carol. I—well—I don't remember. I did mean to tell you though. I was going to. I forgot."

Carol's eyes blazed. "You forgot? Just like that, you forgot? What if I forgot to tell you Aunt Madden would pick up your shoes from the repair shop and you walked all the way down there to get them? What if I forgot about your library books being due? What if I had forgotten last week to tell you Rene picked you to be the information girl at the school booth, and you'd not worn your yellow sweater? I didn't forget. Somehow I don't forget, and you come out looking good. But you forget to tell me things, and I end up getting scolded, or graded down for something, or looking awful at the wrong time. Remember the time you 'forgot' to tell me Jack Lebretti was stopping by to pick up his school papers, and I met him at the door with my hair all in curlers? Well, thanks a lot!"

"Carol, it's disgusting how cross you get. You've got everything."

"What do you mean?"

"You're popular, neat, and smart enough to be in Mr. Fowler's class, and you're a good piano player on top of all that. I wish you wouldn't get so mad. Like I said, I'm sorry. It *was* an accident."

Carol turned to look out the window. The sky was turning pink and purple. A winter twilight. She loved it, but she hated herself for storming at Nina. Poor Nina. She could see how hurt Nina got each time she fussed at her. *Why*, Carol wondered, why do I always promise myself I'll be better, and then I go and blow all my self-control? Carol hated that part about herself. Why did her feelings so often go berserk? What was it about Nina that set her off so?

Millie Norton came into the room. "Why is it dark in here?"

"Look at the sunset, mother."

"Yes, that's beautiful," her mother said. "Remember the old saying, 'red sky at night, sailor's delight'?"

"Another sunny day! Good!" Carol said. "I'm really ready for spring."

"Here, let's turn on a lamp and get things ready for supper. I think I'll turn on that television for a minute and see what the weatherman says we'll have tomorrow."

Millie Norton flicked on the TV and went back to the stove. The announcer pointed at his charts, drew snowflakes in the far west, and big raindrops in the south. "And in our local area," he said, "there is a possibility of some flooding. We're keeping an eye on the rivers and the rapidity of the melt-off. We'll keep you informed."

Carol left him speaking to an empty room. Scooting upstairs she went into her bedroom and found Nina sitting on her bed in the dark.

"What's the matter, Nina?"

"What do you care?"

"Well, I wouldn't have asked you if I didn't want to know."

"Marcia Compton, you know that snotty girl in the seventh grade who always wears that leather quilted-looking vest. Well, she told my teacher I took her five dollars. Mr. Cranston, the principal, called me to the office and asked if I had."

"But you hadn't."

"What do you think? Do you think I'm some kind of thief?"

"Oh, Nina, you must have been so embarrassed."

"I was. I could hardly say anything because I couldn't believe what was happening to me. It was awful. I started to cry right there in Mr. Cranston's office."

"Then what?" Carol sat down on the bed and put her arms around Nina.

"Well, I said I didn't know anything about her money. I hadn't seen her pocketbook. I didn't even know she had any money with her." She began to sob.

"Oh, Nina."

"Then Mr. Cranston said would I—would I 'mind' if he were to check my pockets."

"So?"

"So I stuck my hands in my pockets, and, Carol, the five-dollar bill was there. I could have died."

"How did it get there? Did somebody put it there? What did Mr. Cranston do?"

"He looked at me and told me he was so disappointed. How could I convince him I didn't do it when there it was in my pocket?"

"That Marcia Compton!" Carol was furious. "She's always hated you, and now especially. She couldn't stand it when you were chosen as information girl for the school carnival."

"I don't know, Carol. Honestly. She never liked me, but I didn't know she hated me that much. All I know is Mr. Cranston gave her the money and sent her back to her building or wherever. Then he talked to me."

"What did he say?"

"Oh, he said he'd keep it quiet, and I wouldn't have to tell my parents to come in for an appointment. He said my conscience would punish me, and he said if ever anything else like this happened, he'd have to have a very serious talk with me, the counselors, and my parents. All that stuff."

"What about Marcia?"

"All I know is she turned up her nose and walked out the door like she was some sort of actress. That is, after Mr.

Cranston made me—made me . . . ." Nina's voice sank into a whisper.

"Made you do what?"

"Made me apologize."

"Apologize?"

"Told me I had to apologize to Marcia. I had to say I was sorry I'd taken her money."

"Mr. Cranston!" Carol fumed. "Who does he think he is anyway, that is, other than the principal! Oh, Nina."

Nina leaned against Carol's shoulder. How delicate Nina was. With her wide eyes and pretty short hair, Nina usually seemed happy. Perky, that was the word. But now Carol felt sorry for her. "Have you told mom?" she asked.

"No."

"But you talked to her when you came in."

"Yes. She told me how mad you were at me about the juice on your report."

"You didn't tell her about the money? Marcia? Oh, Nina."

"Carol, I *am* sorry about your paper. I really am."

"That's okay. I was mad. Thank goodness Mr. Fowler had a sense of humor. He said it would be okay."

"I'm glad, Carrie." Sometimes Nina called her that.

Carol felt a lump in her throat.

"Nina."

"What?"

"About that money. How did it get in your pocket? Was it her five dollars or yours?"

Nina was quiet for a minute.

"Well? How did it?"

"It was her money," Nina said in a low voice.

Millie Norton was calling up the stairs, "Girls, come on down. Dinner's almost ready."

"Okay, okay, we're coming," Carol yelled back. She looked at Nina. Had she really heard what Nina said? She didn't dare ask again. She swallowed hard. Those were awful words. She couldn't understand it. Not Nina! No, no! Not her sister, Nina!

"Oh, Nina," was all she could manage to say.

Chapter 3

CAROL looked at her mother. Millie Norton was so busy talking to her dad, for once Carol was glad. Nina had a strained look on her face as she picked at her baked potato.

"Want some butter for your potato?" Millie asked Nina.

"No, thanks."

"She just got some," Carol interrupted. She didn't trust Nina to be normal. She didn't want her parents to know. *I'm ashamed*, she thought. *I'm ashamed for Nina. Ashamed for myself too*, she realized guiltily. *What would people think?* She'd have to cover for Nina. Then her anger flared. Nina, always making life tough! Why should she care? But she did.

"Walt, did you hear about flood warnings?" Millie asked. "The announcer said tonight there is a possibility of some flooding if this snow melts fast."

"Ben Freeburn told me today at the store," Walt said. "Told me the Civil Defense people, I guess, are watching the rivers. A rapid melt-off would probably cause some damage. Let's hope it isn't much. Anyway, we sold seven sump pumps today. Guess people are getting ready, just in case."

"Nina, pass the salt, please," Walt said.

As Nina handed him the shaker that looked like an apple, Carol saw something, a shadow, move outside the door. "What's that?"

"What? Where?" her dad asked.

"There, outside the door."

"I don't see anything, Carol. Besides, it's getting dark out there." He leaned back and reached around for the light switch behind his chair. Turning it on, the Nortons saw just beyond the deck, an opossum staring moodily at them.

"Oh, Walt, look! We've never seen one of those around here before!" Millie jumped up to look.

Carol said, "That's a raccoon, isn't it?"

"No, Carol, raccoons have markings around their eyes. Possums look like this, I think," Millie answered. "I know when I was a child in the South, I could hear the dogs barking when my uncles went coon hunting. Sometimes in the night I think I can still hear the old hounds."

"But those were raccoons, not possums," Walt said.

Before Millie could answer, the opossum, which seemed fixed in a dead stare, looked around. Then in an awkward shuffling manner, he continued down the hill, past Nina's swing set, into the flood plain. From the light on the deck, the Nortons could see the long thin streak at the bottom of the valley where the snow had melted. Although, according to the thermometer, it was freezing again, the streak remained, reminding Carol of a long snake or rope.

"Why isn't it frozen, dad?" she asked.

"The opossum?" her dad said.

"No, no. I mean that streak of water."

"That streak of water has a little current going through it. It'll probably freeze by midnight, but that valley is going to look like Cedar Creek itself twenty-four hours from now if we have nice weather again tomorrow."

"I'm glad it's the weekend," Millie said.

"Me too," Carol said.

They watched the opossum until it was a dark smudge on the far side of the flood plain.

"Get me the dictionary, Nina," Walt Norton said. "I have to find out the difference between a raccoon and an opossum." He found the words and began to explain. "The opossum is small and furry and lives in trees. The raccoon also has a pointed face but has a black mask-like marking under its eyes. The raccoon has a long bushy tail with black rings."

Carol sneaked a look at Nina. Carol couldn't quite fathom the look on Nina's face. Then it came to her. The look in Nina's eyes reminded her of the opossum. Ugly and scared. For a moment it shocked her. It made her feel sick.

"I don't want any dessert," she said. "I've got homework to do."

"Tomorrow is Saturday," Millie said.

"Yeah, I know, but I want to get it done so it won't hang over me." Carol nervously twisted her fingers. "Besides," she added, "I don't want to even think about schoolwork this weekend."

As she went upstairs to her room, she heard her dad saying, "That's Carol for you. Organized. She'll get ahead. Likes to keep at things until they're done."

Carol frowned. Ha! Little did he know! She'd done her homework in school during study hall. She just wanted to be alone. She couldn't stand to sit across from Nina and see that pinched, ugly look on her sister's face. Somehow it made her feel guilty, and she didn't even know why. *Oh, Nina,* she thought, *how could you do this to me?* She lay down on her bed right on top of the quilt her Aunt Madden had made especially for her. Nina would soon come upstairs, and they would have to talk. Nina in the fourth grade. Nina six years younger than she. Carol remembered when she'd watched Nina in the sandbox, when she'd pushed Nina around in her wagon, when she helped Nina learn to ride her bike. Always doing for Nina. And Nina always getting her into binds. Honestly. What if talk starts around school? What if Marcia Compton, that witch, starts rumors about her little thief sister? It had to be a frame. Marcia Compton was just mean enough to do it. But if so, why had Nina admitted the money belonged to Marcia? What really had happened?

"Nina," Carol yelled. "Come here a minute. I've got to ask you something."

"What?" Nina answered from just outside the door.

"What are you doing out there? How long have you been in the hall?"

"I was afraid you wouldn't want me to come in, so I was just sitting on the landing outside the door," Nina said.

"I want to know one thing, Nina. Did you take Marcia's money? If you did, why?"

"I didn't take it, Carol. Honest. I was walking along behind Marcia near the front of the school. She was hurrying to catch the bus to Middle School; you know how they go over there for some of their classes."

"Yeah, yeah. I know. Go on," Carol said.

"Well, the wind was blowing, and she started sneezing," Nina explained. "She reached in her pocket to get a Kleenex, I guess, and the money fell out. I picked it up and tried to call her. She'd already gotten on the bus, so I turned around and went back to my room. I kept the money all day and thought I'd give it to her after school. Meanwhile, during math class, Mr. Cranston came to the door and asked to speak to my teacher, Mrs. Doodle-de-doo. You know—Mrs. Doonsberger."

"Well, what then?"

"Well, next thing I know, Mrs. Doonsberger told me to step into the hall. Mr. Cranston wanted to talk with me. When I did, there was Marcia Compton too. She said I'd taken the money from her pocketbook."

"But you hadn't," Carol sighed.

"You don't understand," Nina said. "I was so scared. I felt so strange. I felt guilty, like maybe I had stolen it or something. And when he told me he wanted to check my pockets, I knew he'd find it, and my face turned red and there it was. The five dollars. And remember, I'd just told him I didn't even know about any money or anything."

"You let Marcia get you! Wait till I see her! Why didn't you just tell him the truth?"

"I meant to give it back, and I did think about it all morning. But during lunch, I kept wondering how it would be if she never knew where it went. If I'd kept it, well, would it have been stealing? I found it, you know."

"Nina, you'll have to tell Mr. Cranston the truth. You can't let him go around thinking you took it from Marcia's pocketbook!"

"He'd never believe me. You should have seen the way he looked at me. Then, when he said he was disappointed, I knew it was over for me."

"And mom and dad? They don't even know."

"Not yet. I don't feel right about it. I know they'll believe me, but what if they don't? And dad. He'll probably blow his top at me. He'll say something about my being too willy-nilly to stand up for what's the truth or something."

"That's not so. You stand up for the truth. We all do. You know how our family is. Truth, honor, all that!"

"But, Carol, if that's so, why couldn't I do it today. I just stood there and couldn't say a word. I felt terrible."

"Even though what you did wasn't wrong, that part was. That is," Carol added, "if you really were planning to give her back the money."

"Well, I was. If I didn't see her this afternoon, I was going to call her tonight and tell her what happened. I really thought she'd be glad to find out she hadn't lost it."

"But you did think about keeping it too."

"Yeah, I know. But Carol, you know I wouldn't have."

"I know. But I also know you can't go around like this until Marcia tells you how she knew you had her money. How did she know?" Carol asked.

"That's just it. I don't know."

"Well, somebody knew. Somebody must have told her. There. See? That person will be able to prove you didn't steal it."

"She wouldn't be able to prove I'd planned to give it back though."

"No, you're right. Honestly, I bet you were terribly embarrassed."

"I still feel embarrassed. My mouth tastes funny." Nina picked at the chenille bedspread and traced around the yellow tulips woven in the pattern.

"Does anyone else know?" Carol asked.

"No, unless Mr. Cranston told old Mrs. Doodle-de-doo."

"And Marcia. No telling what she'll say."

"Yeah, Marcia's that way," Nina said.

"Well, if it makes you feel any better, I'm sorry. You had an awful day."

34

"Thanks, Carrie. I'm glad you believe me. It makes me feel better."

Carol hugged her knees and rocked back and forth for a minute. "Want to go down and have a diet cola with me?"

Nina nodded. "You're good to me, Carrie." She burst into tears.

"What's the matter in there?" Carol's mother called.

"Mother, please come here," Carol answered.

Her mother came in quickly. "Oh my goodness. What's the matter with Nina? What did you say to her?"

"Nothing, mother. Listen to what happened to her today!" Carol put her arm around Nina and listened again. Millie put her arms around them both, and as Nina told her story, for a moment Millie's eyes filled with tears. Then she said firmly, "You've nothing to be ashamed about, Nina. Remember who you are. Don't let things like this pull you down. Truth comes out in the end. Sometimes even I feel guilty in a shop if I notice a sales clerk staring at me. And all I'm doing is browsing. Silly, isn't it?"

"She should talk to Marcia, don't you think, mother?" Carol asked.

"Well, I don't know. I'd like to think about this a bit more." Millie Norton hugged Nina and Carol. "I love you two so much. I wish I could suffer through this old world for you, but the Lord made it so we all have to help carry a bit of the burden. Oh, Nina, you must be strong."

She talked with them some more, and after Nina dried her tears, Carol said, "I'll go get the cola."

Downstairs Carol's dad was reading the paper. "Hi," he said, glancing up. "Where did all of you go? Usually you help your mother clear the table. Where's Millie?"

"I know, dad, but tonight something came up."

"Like what?"

"Oh, like lots of things. I turned in a report this morning that got messed up somehow. Wasn't too bad, though. And Mary Tree announced at lunch she's going to Disney World for spring vacation."

"Good for her."

"Well, no, dad.... she made a federal case about it. Talked about all the other places she's been. Then she asked me where we were going."

"And?"

"I told her we hadn't decided."

"I'll say. We sure haven't." He grinned at her. "Why are you so glum?"

"I'm not glum, dad. I'm just getting a cola."

"You're like a little weather gauge, Carol. I can tell when you're down and out." He put aside his paper. Often he didn't have time to sit and talk, but tonight, he seemed interested.

"Dad," Carol began. "It's about Nina. All day long I was furious at her. She spilled orange juice on my Jupiter report, and I'd really wanted to get an 'A' on it. I worked hard to make it look neat. All day I couldn't wait until I got my hands on her. I was so mad!"

"My goodness, what where you planning to do?" Walt Norton asked.

"I don't know. Shake her. Something. I was really mad."

"And?"

"Well, tonight she told me Marcia Compton accused her of stealing a five-dollar bill from her pocketbook. She hadn't done it. She's been going around feeling awful all day. I'm sorry I felt so mean toward her."

"Oh my, honey, feelings are something else, aren't they? Makes us know how human we are. Where's Nina?"

"Upstairs with mom."

"She told Millie?"

"Yeah."

"Let's go up there for a minute and talk."

"Thanks, dad."

They took glasses and another diet cola and went upstairs.

"Here we are. Let's talk." Walt Norton always came to the point. "Nothing like a good talk."

"Oh, daddy," Nina said, looking up.

"This is what families are for," Walt said.

"But lots of families don't know about this part," Carol added.

"A family shares each other's troubles. They don't just eat and sleep in the same house," Millie said.

The Nortons sat together on the side of Nina's bed and sipped cola from their funny old Flintstone jelly glasses. Soon they started talking about other things, and Nina began to relax.

Carol stood up and walked to the window. Stars twinkled above the treeline, and somehow, deep inside, Carol felt grateful it was Friday night. For once there wasn't a basketball game or anything else scheduled. Instead, they had just been together. It was a good feeling.

Later, after Nina turned out her lamp, Carol sat looking through one of her magazines. She liked looking at the fashions, reading about beauty ideas and tips. She liked doing the quizzes. One was entitled "What Do You Really Know About Yourself?" Carol decided to read the directions.

Which answer best describes your reaction to the following situations:

    1. You have been told you may be nominated as class delegate

to the student council. (a) You act as though you deserve the nomination. (b) You pretend you haven't heard about it. (c) You tell your closest friends. (d) You begin to plan your campaign.

Carol circled "c" and went on to the next question.

2. You've been told your uncle left you a fortune. (a) You decide to give it to charity. (b) You plan a wild shopping spree. (c) You plan a huge celebration for your classmates. (d) You decide to save it for your future career plans.

Carol stopped to think. *Would I really want to share it? Maybe I should save it. Maybe I'm a little selfish,* she thought, *but it would be fun to blow it all on a shopping spree.* She chewed the top of the eraser. *This is really silly,* she thought. *I can't answer this one. It isn't realistic, just something to make me not know who I am or how I feel.* Suddenly she was disgusted by the whole idea. Somebody probably got paid a fortune just to think up such a dumb quiz. Taking her pencil, she marked a big cross over the entire page, and wrote "DUMB!" in every space.

Slipping her feet into her fuzzy slippers, she turned out the light and padded over to the window. She looked out toward Cedar Creek. From her upstairs window she could see moonlight glimmering on the water. It was high and wavy. She realized with a start that she'd never seen it so high before. The idea of a flood struck her as a possibility. Not probable but possible. Oh, well. Let somebody else worry about all that.

She hurried back to her bed and slipped under the warm covers. As she floated off to sleep, she heard the phone ring, and downstairs, her dad moved to answer it. "Sure, Jake, I'll be glad to help. I'll come right away."

Chapter 4

SATURDAY was a gorgeous day. "I can't believe this," Carol said, stretching. "Two sunny days in a row!"

"That's hard to believe this time of year in Indiana."

"Yeah, but don't knock it, Nina. We had it coming."

"I'll take this anyday. Oh, Carol, guess what?"

"What?"

"Today's Saturday."

"So?"

"Maybe I can play outside."

"Ha! Maybe the sun is shining, but I'll bet it won't melt the snow. There's enough snow out there to last till summer!"

"Mama told me to remind you about Mrs. Bailey."

"Mrs. Bailey? You mean that meeting is today?"

"I don't have to go, do I, Carol?"

"If I have to, you've got to go. I don't see why either of us has to go. Some dumb meeting."

"I wish mama would stop getting us involved in her stuff. What's it about anyway?"

"I don't know. Something about her club planning a Mother-Daughter banquet. They want a few girls in on the planning part. I'm going to try to get out of it. Somebody else can plan the thing. Besides, I don't even want to go to the stupid banquet."

"I had a good time last year, Carol. Remember they had a magician?"

"I'm going downstairs and protest," Carol said, putting on her robe.

"Mom," she called, "remember I have to work on my science project today? I really can't go to Mrs. Bailey's house. Not today."

"You'll go just like you said you would, Carol. Besides, it won't take more than an hour."

"Mother!" Carol complained. "Why can't you and your committee do it alone? Why doesn't dear Mrs. Ellen Hartly do something? Her girls never do anything. It's always us."

"You promised you'd do this for me at least a month ago."

"That was in the middle of February, mother, and it was snowing."

"And we didn't have anything else to do," Nina added.

"Well, I don't ask you often. It won't hurt for you to volunteer once in a while."

"But we did it last year too."

"And we had the best Mother-Daughter banquet we've ever had. See what you girls did last year?" Millie smiled. "After all, you only have to offer some opinions. Nothing much except sit there and be polite. It won't hurt you one bit to put out for me for a change."

"Mother, I wanted to go roller skating with Kathy," Nina

said. She spread the butter on her toast, took a big bite, and raised her eyebrows knowingly at Carol.

"Yeah," said Carol, taking the clue. "I wanted to finish my school project."

"Nina, you can't roller skate today. The sidewalks aren't even clear. And Carol, if I remember right, you just got your science project list two days ago."

"Mom, I have to decide what project to do. So, maybe I'm not quite ready to 'finish' it yet."

Millie laughed. "I'll say you aren't. And Nina, just how did you plan to roller skate?"

"Kathy is going to the roller rink with her sister. I thought maybe you'd let me go."

"No, honey. I can't. You know that."

"But why?"

"She goes with that Gerry somebody, and they don't even go skating. He's been in trouble ever since he was in junior high."

"He doesn't even go to school anymore," Nina volunteered. "He's got a job somewhere."

"Some job," Carol said. "He sweeps out the arcade."

"So, he sweeps out the arcade. Somebody's got to do it."

"That's not the point," Millie said. "That can be a worthwhile job, nothing whatsoever wrong with that. But you know, girls, he's doing it only until his court trial comes up. Come on, girls, you're straining at a gnat."

"Please, mother. I haven't gone roller skating in an age."

"No, not under those circumstances. We take you there, you know that. But, I won't let you go with Kathy and her sister and that boy."

"But what about Kathy? What's going to happen to her?" Nina asked.

"I don't know. I hope nothing happens to her. She's a

sweet girl, and maybe she'll be wise enough to learn from what her sister's doing. I don't think they should let those girls run around so unsupervised."

"Some people don't think like you do, mother," Carol said. "They let their kids grow up."

"That's their prerogative," Millie said flatly. "Why not ask Kathy to come over here? Your dad will be here and you two can play while Carol and I scoot over to Mrs. Bailey's."

"You mean Nina doesn't have to go? Mother, that's not fair. Can't I stay and watch Nina and Kathy?"

"Carol, come on. Try to be a little more understanding."

"Boy, that really makes me cross," Carol said. "Nina, you lucky duck!" She knew she couldn't talk her mother out of it. "After all the things I've done for you, too," she grumbled. Somehow breakfast didn't seem half as good as it usually did on Saturdays.

Nina had already dialed Kathy and was saying, "... and why don't you bring your records too?"

The highway seemed like a ribbon of gray between mounds and ruts of melting ice. In some places the ice was slushy and in other places, especially the heavily trampled pathways, Carol could see ragged patches and tinges of green. Carol stared morosely out of the window. Her mother drove cautiously. Coming to the First Street Bridge, it surprised Carol and Millie how many people were milling back and forth by the railing. Then they saw why.

"Look at the creek, mom!" Carol said. "Look how high the water is! That's incredible!"

Her mother drove carefully over the bridge, peering out the window.

"My, my, look at that current," she exclaimed.

"Do you think it will go over the bank?" Carol asked.

"If we continue to have a rapid melt-off, all this snow has to go somewhere. I don't know, but I hope it doesn't melt too fast."

Somehow it seemed strange and exciting to see the creek water rushing so hard beneath them. A few yards beyond the bridge, they saw a huge puddle spreading all the way across the intersection.

"This is a low spot," Millie commented. "I hope it hasn't gotten too deep for us to go through."

Another car came slowly toward them. The people inside were craning their necks, looking at the water in the road. They smiled and waved as their car slowly passed making a funny whooshing noise, water spraying out on all sides.

"It seems like the water is right under my feet," Carol said.

"It certainly is high," her mother agreed.

Soon they passed the intersection and drove a few more blocks and turned right. They pulled up to a huge soggy-looking snowbank and parked.

"Watch your step, Carol," Millie Norton said. "I'm glad we wore our boots. It's almost like a lake out here."

"Oh, wow! Mother, look at this. The slush is all the way up to my ankles!"

They picked their way through the icy, watery mess and rang Mrs. Bailey's doorbell.

"Any trouble getting here?" Mrs. Bailey's voice called out. "Lots of water out there. Look over there." She pointed down the street in the other direction.

"What's that?" Carol asked.

She could see water gushing out of a rain basin. It looked like a pipe had broken.

"The sewers and drains can't carry it off fast enough," Mrs. Bailey said. "It backs up and," she paused, "see how it looks like a fountain, almost like a fire hydrant that's been opened."

"Will that affect your house? Get in your basement or something?" Millie asked.

"Probably not. It tends to run the other way down Van Buren. Of course I'm not saying the whole place might not flood. Never can tell, the way the radio and television announcers are talking." Mrs. Bailey laughed pleasantly. "Let's not worry yet. Come on in."

They went into a room decorated beautifully with antiques and several built-in china closets.

"I just love antique china," Millie said. Carol looked at the room and loved the way the warm sun streamed in, making the cut glass vase cast sparkles on the rug. She found a soft blue velvet chair and sat down.

"This won't take but about thirty or forty minutes," Mrs. Bailey said cheerfully. "We just want to make sure our plans will appeal to adults and you young people alike." The clocks ticked softly and the warm sun made Carol feel lazy. A few more people came, and before long they were busily discussing decorations, spring flowers that might be available for centerpieces, and program ideas. It wasn't a long meeting, and Carol didn't really mind being there. After all, she thought, what could she do outside with all that water and slush around?

As they drove home, Carol and her mother were amazed. In less than one hour, water seemed everywhere. Barricades had been placed several yards from the intersection at First and Cedar. The bridge was closed. The street overflowing.

"We just came this way, mother," Carol said in astonishment. "Look at all this water!"

Millie began to back up. "Wow! We'll have to go around by Seventh Street. I didn't realize it was rising so fast."

44

The springlike weather was inviting, and people were out-side even though it was slushy and messy to walk. The air felt mild, just wonderful. "It's great not to have to wear a bulky coat," Carol said. "I just love this."

Their street was soggy and slushy, but the snow had melted off the driveway just enough for the Nortons to have a little path to the mailbox.

Coming into the house, Carol couldn't wait to tell Nina and Kathy about the bridge.

"No kidding," Kathy exclaimed. "How will I get home?"

"Don't worry, we'll get you over there. We'll have to go by Seventh Street. It's open," Millie said. "Are you two hav-ing a good time?"

"Oh, yes," the girls answered and went on with their play.

Carol went to her room to change into her jeans. Saturday afternoon, and the day was shot as far as she was concerned. Yesterday, a messy report, Nina's problem with Marcia, and that wasn't over yet. No doubt she'd hear a lot more about that at school on Monday. Today—messing around with her mother's club meeting. "Rats," she said aloud. "It just isn't fair. I'm sick of all this. I think I'll call Reba or Janice or somebody. Anybody will do. Even Mary Tree, if nobody else is home."

Suddenly it seemed good to have something to do. Reba would want to talk about Dick Moore—that stuffed shirt. Janice would probably brag about Mr. Fowler's grades, and Mary Tree, well, no telling what juicy tidbit she might have. Carol decided to call Mary Tree.

"May as well gossip with Mary," she said to her mirror. "I can't stand all that drivel the others have to say."

She ran downstairs, grabbed a couple of chocolate chip cookies from the cookie can, and called, "Don't bother me for a minute, mom. I'm gonna use the phone."

"Don't tie it up for long, honey," her mother called from the laundry room.

"Okay." Carol curled up in the stuffed chair by the phone and dialed Mary Tree.

"Hi." Mary was ready to talk.

"What's new?" Carol wanted to know.

"Nothing much. Just some good juicy gossip."

"Oh, good! Who's it about?" Carol bit into her cookie.

"Want to guess?"

"Reba? Dick Moore? I don't know."

"Guess again," Mary Tree said.

"Who, me?" Carol said, half joking.

"Yes."

"Me? I haven't done anything."

"That's not what I heard today." Mary Tree sounded like she was teasing, but Carol began to feel uncomfortable.

"What did you hear, and who said it?" Carol demanded.

"Nothing much. Just one little thing."

"Just one little thing like what?" Carol was getting angry.

"Oh," Mary Tree said airily, "that you are selfish about a few things."

"Selfish? You must be crazy!" Carol was furious. "What have I been selfish about?"

"Oh, about not wanting to do any of the work when it comes to planning the Spring Fun Day. All you wanted was to get your name on the planning committee, but when they asked you to make phone calls or collect things for the Crazy Auction, you refused."

"I refused? Who said? I didn't refuse."

"That's for you to guess and me to know."

"Mary Tree! You're mean. I don't have to listen to this!" Carol was steamed.

"Oh, come on, Carol," Mary was trying again. "I just

heard you hedged a lot when Johnny McKee asked you to help with the auction."

"So?"

"So, if it's true, why are you so mad? What difference does it make?"

"I didn't want to be on Johnny's committee, because— well, because...." Carol blurted.

"Well, because why?"

"That's for you to guess and for me to know!" Carol answered cagily. For once it was nice to turn the tables on Mary. So let Mary Tree wonder about that! It would be just enough to get Mary Tree started again.

"Mary, I've got to go. Mom needs me in the kitchen. Besides, I'm getting tired of this. All I called you for was to ask when you're leaving for Florida. You're going, right?"

"That's right. Uncle Jason and Aunt Tildy are going down. They asked me to go along. Mom didn't care . . . so."

"You're lucky." Carol felt a twinge of envy.

"Why did you want to know when I was leaving, anyway?"

"Oh, nothing really. I just wondered," Carol admitted. She really wasn't interested in Mary's trip. She just hadn't felt like talking with Reba or Janice.

"What about you? Where is your family going? Have they decided yet?"

"We, ah, we haven't talked about it much." Carol hesitated. She knew they planned nothing special. Maybe they'd go shopping or maybe she'd spend a night or two with her Aunt Madden, see a movie, or swim at the Y. Suddenly Carol felt a bit ashamed to admit her family probably wouldn't be doing anything. Spending a night or so with her Aunt Madden seemed like peanuts compared to Mary Tree's trip to Disney World.

"I don't think we'll do anything this year. Not that I know of, not yet, at least," Carol said defensively.

Mary Tree laughed. "So, you're free as a goose. You know something," she added. "That's not all bad."

"What do you mean?" Carol asked.

"Well," Mary confided. "I don't have the chance to just stay at home and do nothing. Do you know something?"

"What?"

"Well, my folks don't care a fig about staying home. They're always going, flitting around. I don't think they know how to stay home."

"People are different," Carol volunteered. "Sounds exciting to me though. Wish my family liked to travel. Honestly, do you know I've never been anywhere except the State Fair in Indianapolis? I've never been to Chicago, Toledo, or Detroit."

"Greenfield Village? You've been there, haven't you?"

"Oh, yes, back in the fifth grade when we all went as a class. That's it, though."

"Carol, you have *got* to get around."

"I know, I know. I'm going to die of boredom. I'm going to die before ever having been anywhere. Do you realize, Mary, I've never even seen a famous person?"

"Is that a fact? You really have been deprived, Carol. I've seen lots of famous people—rock stars, comedians, all that stuff."

"Yeah, I know, but you get to go to some of those fancy concerts and plays with your relatives. You go to Chicago."

"With Uncle Jason and Aunt Tildy. That's who."

"Well, at least you get to go. You get around. I don't even get to stay up and watch the late movies!" Carol pretended to laugh, but inside, she felt different. It was really horrible the way her folks were.

48

"Got to go, Mary. Mom will get me if I hang on too long. You know how parents can be. Really, really limiting!"

"No, hey, wait a minute, Carol," Mary hurried.

"Why?"

"Because I want to ask you if you think your parents would let you go to Florida, to Disney World, with me? Uncle Jason and Aunt Tildy said I could ask somebody to go along."

"Me? You're kidding? I'd love it! I really would love to go!" Carol could hardly believe her ears!

"Well, then ask your parents. Let me know."

Chapter 5

"OH, MOTHER, just think! Disney World! Can I? Can I go?"

"I don't know, dear. I'll have to talk it over with your dad. Besides, I didn't know you and Mary Tree were such good friends."

"You know Mary, don't you, mom? They live over on Woodbridge. Her mom's got that fancy job in Fort Wayne, a buyer for some woman's shop, remember?"

"What about her dad?"

"I don't know. Her dad left her mother several years ago."

"Who stays with Mary during the day?" her mother asked.

"Nobody. She stays at a neighbor's house sometimes. Mostly she stays after school until the four-thirty bus and gets home about an hour before her mom does."

"I'd hate that arrangement," her mother said quietly.

"I don't think she has much choice, mom. Her mother has to work."

"What do you mean has to work? She's old man Bradbury's daughter, and he left her a mint."

"Mother, I know she has the money. That's not it. Mary says she has to work because of her mind, her nerves, whatever you want to call it."

"Well, fine, but I knew it wasn't money. The whole town knows about Bradbury's money. She works because she's bored at home, is that it?"

"Well, mother, if all you did all day was play bridge, tennis, golf, or shop, wouldn't you get bored after a while?"

"Actually, no. I think I'd enjoy doing some of those things. I just wish I had more of a chance to do them. You girls keep me hopping." Millie chuckled, "I'll have you know I once could play a very good game of golf."

"That's not it, mom, and you know it. You work because we need the money."

"Well, if we didn't have the money, we'd get along somehow. But I do hope my part-time job at the hospital will help cover part of your schooling some day."

"Mom, do you think maybe I could go with Mary? Her Aunt Tildy and Uncle Jason are going. They're the ones who practically raise Mary. Please?"

"Carol, I don't know. I honestly don't. I have to discuss this with your dad. I'd like to know a little more about Mary. I know Tildy Grady is Mary's mother's sister, a Bradbury." Millie Norton was busy fixing the salad.

"Mother does it matter who Tildy Grady is or was before she married? I mean do you really have to study her family tree or something? Mary asked me to go. They've got the money. They just want me to go along and be company for Mary. Besides, Mary is my friend."

"She's a gossip," Nina chimed in. "Everybody in school knows how she likes to make up things about people."

"Well, so what? Lots of people gossip. I like to gossip. That's not so bad."

"Girls, girls," Millie cautioned. "I'm sure she's nice. All I'm saying is I'd like to meet her a time or two and see what she's like. Sounds like she's pretty rudderless."

"Rudderless!" Carol wailed. "I can't believe you're saying this, mother. She's just independent. You just don't know her. I know her real well. She's okay. Please, please let me go. I never go anywhere. I've never been anywhere. Do you want me to live a sheltered life and never do anything? Here I am practically grown up, and I've never had any opportunities. Even Aunt Madden said it would be good for me to travel. Remember when we were talking about the exchange student?"

"Aunt Madden says everyone should be an exchange student. She was," Millie answered. "She loves to travel."

"Mother, see there. Some people just travel more than others. I'd like to travel. I haven't been anywhere. I've been to Greenfield Village and Indianapolis. That's all!"

"You went to Madison one time," Nina said.

"Madison, Indiana! Can you believe that? Yeah, the fall church tour. Mother," Carol continued, "this just can't be. I'm the only one in the whole school who's never been anywhere south of Madison. Even Reba has been to Louisville. It's disgraceful!"

"You went with me to South Carolina one time, remember?"

"Mother, I must have been seven years old! That doesn't count."

"That's enough for now, Carol. I'll talk it over with your dad. We'll discuss it and let you know."

52

"Mother, I can't believe this. You aren't even excited about my chance to go. Here I am with a way to see the United States, and you act like it's nothing. I just don't understand." Carol slammed the napkins on the table.

"Carol, that's enough."

"Yes, ma'am."

Carol straightened a fork and glared at Nina. Then she thought of something. "Mother, could Mary Tree spend the night over here? It would give you a chance to meet her."

"Carol, I—I—I guess so."

"Okay, okay, mother."

"But why not? Go ahead. Ask her. That would help me get to know her a little better."

Carol hesitated. It might not be such a good idea after all, she thought. It sure would give her folks a chance to know Mary, but if Mary started her snippy talk and her high and mighty way of lording it over everybody, they just might not let her go.

"I'll think about it, mom." Carol didn't want anything to mess up her chance to go to Disney World. Suddenly it seemed to be the most important thing in her whole life!

On Sunday, the sky wasn't clear, but the sun seemed to slip in and out of the clouds. Looking at the flood plain, Carol thought it strange to be looking down on the huge lake that had formed right behind her house. She pushed open the window. The smell of spring—moist, earthy, and fragrant, made her want to wear something light and color-ful to church. If she were younger, she'd like to run and roll in the grass. That is, she thought ironically, if there was any grass. She longed to run, to fling her arms out in the wind. She loved spring. But, as she picked out her pink blouse, a color that reminded her of Easter eggs, she realized it was still cold outside. She pulled down the window and reached for her sweater. Well, I won't wear my coat, she decided.

Nina came hurrying into the room. "You've got ten minutes before we leave for church. Hurry up."

"Okay," Carol said, brushing her hair. She liked the way her shiny brown hair bounced. Some days she felt positively drab, but today she felt bright and good. "I'm not so bad looking," she said to herself. She had to admit she usually looked sharp. Reba always complained about wearing stocking hats, but Carol wore hers with a lot of style. In fact, she had several hat and scarf sets, and she especially liked the knitted and crocheted designs. Carol fixed her favorite ski hat so that it had just the right look.

"Good Aunt Madden," she said. "What would she do if she didn't have us to knit and crochet for?"

Nina laughed. "Maybe she'd clean her house or cook or garden."

"You know Aunt Madden couldn't cook a pot of chili without asking mom how much salt to put in it," Carol answered.

"Well, that doesn't bother me. I'd survive anyway."

"On what?" Carol asked.

"On restaurant food. That's what Aunt Madden does."

"I'd travel. I wouldn't stay home. I'd visit every country in the world."

"Then you'd come home and do what she does. She raves and raves about mom's good homecooked meals. You'd think she was starved."

"She is starved, silly." Suddenly Carol felt sober. "I think she is starved—for family. I think she does all that traveling so she won't have to stare at the walls."

"How could anyone ever just do that anyway?" Nina asked, straightening the cuff on her blouse.

"I don't know. Some people get depressed when they get

older. Especially if they're like Aunt Madden. She doesn't really do much except crochet. That is, when she's not on one of her tours."

"Sounds like a great way to live, if you ask me," Nina said. They hurried down the stairs, and Nina called, "Hey, wait for us!"

"Millie," Mr. Norton said as he backed the car down the driveway, "We'll have to go by the Ninth Street Bridge. They've closed Seventh Street."

"Why? Do you mean the water's that high?" Millie sounded concerned.

"They're worried about the water washing away the concrete foundations. That bridge was supposed to be re-built next year, but if it washes out, they'll have to build it before then. I hope not," Walt added. "We've got enough problems in this area without added expenses."

"People are so hard hit, economically," Millie said. "I just don't know what some of them are going to do. I never thought this recession or depression or whatever those economists want to call it would last this long."

Carol listened. She knew it was hard for everyone. People were out of jobs, laid off, and struggling to make ends meet. How thankful she was her folks were still working. "Glad you've got your job, dad," she said.

"Oh, yes, but things at the lumberyard are really slow. Like I said, everybody is affected. High interest rates, unemployment, taxes. I don't know. I get worried."

"And now the flood. Well, it isn't a flood yet," Carol said.

"It may not seem like a flood yet, but things are getting serious. The St. Mary's River is supposed to crest in a day or so, and the St. Joseph's River is already close to flood stage. The Maumee River is around 23 feet, and that's high. It's scary," Walt said.

"Dad, is that why they call Fort Wayne the city of three rivers?" Nina asked.

"Yes, aren't you forgetting the Three Rivers Festival? We went to it last June. Why do you think they named it the Three Rivers Festival?"

"Yeah, that was fun, dad. I remember. Remember that silly river raft race?"

"Do they have that festival every year?" Carol asked.

"Yes. That and the Johnny Appleseed Festival. And there's an old Historic Fort and the art museum which are nice to visit. It's a pretty swell place, Fort Wayne is, don't you think?" Walt said.

"I'm glad we live in our town, though," Nina piped up. "I like it here."

"Yes, but Fort Wayne is a really great place to live, or at least live near," Millie said. "I like being able to go there to shop, see plays, take in the Philharmonic sometimes. And Fort Wayne has some good restaurants."

"Well, we have an ACT I theater group," Carol said.

"Yes and it's good too," Walt said.

"And an Auburn Community Band," Nina added.

"And that's good too," Millie agreed.

"Oh, well, I like the city, but it's nice to live here. It's great to know your neighbors, feel secure, and you know, there's a friendly spirit here," Millie said, looking all the while at the huge lakelike puddles they were cautiously driving through.

"People probably feel that way everywhere," Carol said.

"No, they don't," Walt said. "People get caught up in their own problems and sometimes don't realize the drama taking place right outside their door. Auburn is a fantastic place to live, and there's plenty going on."

"Especially around Labor Day Weekend when all the old

56

Auburns, Cords, and Duesenberg cars come back for their annual parade," Millie said.

"I love to see those cars," Nina said. "I wish I had one."

"And just to think, they were made right here," Carol said.

The Nortons talked about the neighboring towns and decided every little place had its appeal. "It's the people that make a place. People need people whether they're in Chicago or Little Rock, South Carolina."

"Little Rock, South Carolina, is just a crossroads."

"It's got a post office, Nina," Carol said. "Besides, it does have a rock. I saw it one time."

"Yeah, painted white. I remember," Nina said.

"It's not the rock you go to see, silly, it's the family," Millie said. "I don't care where the family is; it can be Catfish Creek or Las Vegas, Nevada. People need family."

"Yeah, but not everybody has one," Carol said.

"Well, that's true," Millie said. "But they can reach out to people. Some friends are closer than family."

"Depression and loneliness is a pretty awful thing," Walt said.

"Is Aunt Madden depressed?" Nina asked.

"Aunt Madden? Why do you ask that?" Millie said.

"Because Carol said Aunt Madden travels all the time just so she won't stay depressed."

"We all get depressed some time or other, but some people can't snap out of it like others do. They need extra help."

"What about Aunt Madden?" Nina asked again.

"I don't know. I think maybe she does. She's so sensitive and her health isn't good."

"I don't think that's it," Carol said. "I think she needs to be needed."

"Well, I need her," Nina said.

"We're going to see her after church," Walt said. "How's that?"

"Look at that water!" Carol could hardly believe her eyes. The water surging under the Ninth Street Bridge was practically level with the ground.

"I can't believe that, mom. It might go in those houses!"

"Yes, it could. Some people already have water in their basements," Walt said. "Jake Littlejohn has about two feet of water in his."

"I'm glad we live on a hill," Nina said.

"Yes, we are lucky. So far our basement is dry," Walt commented.

They passed over the bridge with its bulging current just beneath and nodded at the people standing nearby, mostly men wearing long wading boots. Some were near the edge, and one man had a boat pulled up on the bank.

"Where does Cedar Creek go?" Carol asked.

"It flows right into the St. Joe River," her dad answered. "That's the same creek that runs along the back of our property. It's a good thing the flood plain is out there."

They parked at the church, and Carol saw Reba and also Dick. She waved. She hoped she'd see Eldon Lewiston. As Nina ran on ahead of her parents and opened the door, Carol heard an unfamiliar sound. Looking around and up, she saw nothing but gray clouds scudding fast and low across the sky. The wind was raw and cut through her. She wished she'd worn her coat. She heard the unfamiliar call again.

Then she saw it. A lone Canada goose, flying just above the leafless treetops, honking a lonely desperate call. He flew, almost brushing the tops of the snapping limbs, just beneath those gray clouds, moving through splashes of sunlight, crying his hoarse haunting call. Was he lost? Looking for his mate? Trying to find or catch up with his flock? It was an eerie sound, that honking. Carol remembered a story where a writer described flying geese as looking like flying frying pans. That's it, she thought, an awkward flying frying pan. It was funny but beautiful, and there was a sadness about it. The lone Canada goose was moving fast, right overhead, straight toward the courthouse square. Carol felt she could almost touch him, and somehow she seemed to understand the urgency of his flight.

"Oh, Carol," Nina said. "Come on." She'd poked her head out of the door and was calling. "We're waiting."

"Nina!" Carol said. "I just saw a Canada goose, flying toward the courthouse."

"So maybe he was lost," Nina said. "Come on."

Carol sat through church and later spoke to Reba. Dick came up behind them and teased, "You have your canoe ready, Carol? There's going to be river behind your house by tonight."

"So far all we have is a lake. Thank goodness our basement is dry."

"Great," Reba said. "We've got the pump going, trying to get water out of ours. Not much has gotten in yet."

"We're sure watching our place," Dick said. "Our house is on low ground, and if the creek floods, we'll get it."

"What will you do?" Carol asked.

"Sandbag or something."

"Sandbag? What does that really mean?"

"Well," Dick and Reba explained, "sandbagging is when you fill a bag with sand, not too full, not too little, just loose enough to let it be floppy. Then when you pile one bag on the others, it forms a kind of wall."

"Sounds like a lot of work," Carol said. "I'm glad I don't have to think about that."

"Like I said, Carol," Reba pointed out, "you're lucky. Keep your fingers crossed for us. Things are supposed to get worse. If they do, we may have to evacuate."

"Evacuate? You mean leave your house? Really? That seems unreal. Not here in our town!"

"Yes, really," Dick said. "People who live in low-lying areas may have to think about that whether they want to or not."

"What will you do, Reba, if you have to?" Carol asked. The wind was getting stronger, and she turned up the collar of her raincoat. "I should have worn my winter coat," she grumbled.

"We'll go to my Uncle's house," Reba said. "Thank goodness he doesn't live far away."

"What about you, Dick?"

"I don't know." He was more serious than Carol had ever seen him.

"Well, I've got to go," Carol said. "We're stopping by to see Aunt Madden. Mother said she wants to talk to us."

Carol kicked a pile of melting ice to get her footing as she scrambled to get to the car. It splashed into the muddy water. "Uukk. Messy," she said.

I'll bet Disney World people wouldn't even know what this dirty junk ice stuff looks like, she thought. *I've got to get away from here. I hate this stuff. I hate this weather. I hate it.*

"Let's go, dad," she said, settling into the car. She remembered the goose. Oh, to be able to lift one's wings and skim above the treetops! There was something haunting about what she'd seen. She wished she knew where it was headed. Had it reached its destination? Had it found a safe place? She felt uneasy. She wasn't sure why.

Chapter 6

AUNT MADDEN met them at the door. She was thin and angular. "Oh, you girls, how good to see you!" She seemed happy, her eyes bright and shiny. She reached out and hugged them.

"Please, please come in. Walt, let's have some coffee. Millie, you'd rather have tea, wouldn't you? I just put the kettle on. I didn't quite know exactly when to expect you. After church, I know you said, but I didn't know what time. I've been pacing around here waiting."

The words poured out, Carol's aunt moving around, straightening napkins, reaching for the spiced tea, finding spoons, handing Walt the morning paper, pointing where the girls should put their coats and sweaters.

"Right here, Carol. Let me take that sweater and put it up for you."

"I can do it, Aunt Madden," Carol said, reaching for a hanger.

"Nina, get your dad and mother some nice cups and saucers. China ones, honey. They're in the cupboard."

"Slow down, Madden," Walt said. "Millie, can't you make Madden take things a little easier?" he teased.

"You know I would if I could," Millie answered. "She's always been the high-strung one, haven't you, Madden?"

"Oh, dear, you know I'd sit and hold my hands if I could. I just can't. I tried it one time, and I broke out in a rash. Hives, that's what it was. The doctors told me to take up needlework. Look at my fingers, Millie. Have you ever seen such pricked fingers? I've been embroidering lately. Remember the quilts we saw in Shipshewana? I ordered one of those kits. Well, I've been putting it off for such a long time, and I said to myself the other night, Madden, it's time you got off your old duff and got busy doing something beautiful. *Beautiful*, do you get that word, Nina? A person has to have beauty in her life. Don't you ever forget it."

Carol watched her mother. Aunt Madden seemed unusually high strung. Would her parents stay long? It sometimes bothered her dad when Aunt Madden kept up her incessant talk.

Her parents sat at the round table in the kitchen. She joined them. Nina sat on the sofa and leafed through some magazines.

"Aunt Madden," Carol said, "do you remember Mary Tree? She asked me to go to Disney World with her."

"She did? That's wonderful, just wonderful! Of course you'll go! Of course you will! Every girl ought to have an opportunity like that. Travel. That's so important. Walt, I've told you and Millie a hundred times you've got to get these girls out and about. See the USA. Nothing like it. Gives you a sense of who you are. Makes you think about where your roots are. The more you travel, the more you know where you're from. And, you get to be a citizen of the world! Not just some little burg in the middle of America! This is a great and wonderful country in which to live!" She emphasized each word as though preparing to recite a speech, all the while pouring tea for Millie and coffee for Walt.

"And whatever shall I give you Carol? Milk? Pop? Some hot lemonade?"

"Hot lemonade? Uukk! That would be terrible," the girls said.

Aunt Madden laughed, "No, honey, the more you travel the more you realize what seems strange to you isn't in other places. Why in the South, I could give you some sassafras tea. I tell you what, I'll give you some orange juice. That's what I'll do. I bought some the other day. There was a sale on, and I picked up five cans of this frozen stuff. I'll fix you some right now."

"Madden," Carol's mother said, "Sit down. Carol and Nina can do the orange juice."

"Yeah, don't worry about us, Aunt Madden. I bet I make the orange juice more than you know," Carol said.

"Yeah, she makes it every morning, don't you?" Nina scoffed.

"Ha! I make it more than you do."

"Girls." Walt gave them a look, and they settled down.

Carol mixed the orange juice and watched a cardinal peck at sunflower seeds on the damp patio. A few nuthatches were busy at the feeder.

She listened to her parents, "Madden, you must calm down. It isn't that bad, is it?" her mother was asking.

"Oh, yes, it is, Millie. You don't understand. I just feel so bad about it. And I get to sitting here watching television, my fingers going as fast as they can, and I try to stay calm. I really do, but I get so worked up. Things get to me."

"Madden, why don't you just turn the thing off?" Carol's dad said.

"I can't, Walt. I can't. I turn it off, then I pace around here and worry about what I'm not seeing. So I snap it on again and there I go again."

"Well, you can't solve all the evils of the world," Millie soothed.

"They shouldn't show those things on television, anyway," Walt said.

"Well, I'm not saying they shouldn't show them," Aunt Madden said. "I'm just saying they shouldn't show them like that! Crying, bloated stomachs, flies all over their eyes. Dying in the sand. It's inhuman!"

"Starvation is inhuman, Madden."

"I know, Millie, but I think they're poisoning us. In our minds. Our heads, you understand. I go to bed and I see those children. I can't stand it."

"Maddie, you're more susceptible than some. Knowing that, you should turn off the set. Get involved in something else." Walt shook his head. "I'm sympathetic, but you've got to know how much you can take."

"Oh, Walt, it's a torment. I can't rest."

"Madden," Carol's mother said gently, "Do you think it's because you were trained to be a nurse? You know too much about suffering."

"If I could just get that job back," Madden blurted out. "With the demand for nurses so high, I ought to be able to have a job. If I just hadn't had that breakdown."

"You were stressed, Madden. Too tired." Millie sipped her tea. "All that traveling last time wore you out. Then you had that bout with the flu."

"You just wouldn't rest," Walt reminded her.

Carol came back to the table and sat down.

"I'll fix some sandwiches. You're probably starving," Aunt Madden said.

"No, I'm not, Aunt Madden. I'll just nibble on a few of these peanuts." Carol picked up a few nuts. "Actually, Aunt Madden," she volunteered, "you should learn to take life easy and enjoy all this relaxing."

"No, she shouldn't," Nina said looking up. "If that old television makes her nervous, she should get rid of it. Go work for the Salvation Army, the Red Cross, or something."

"Well, you're right, Nina," Carol said looking at her sister with surprise.

"Just because you had a nervous breakdown doesn't mean you can't do things anymore," Millie said. "You have to pace yourself."

"Who wants an old bag like me?" Madden said, half joking. "They'd say, who's that old bag coming down the pike, coming to take care of me?" It struck her as funny and she laughed. Carol was glad her aunt didn't burst into tears like she sometimes did, especially when she'd say something sarcastic about herself.

"At least you're a thin bag," Millie laughed. "If I were to go somewhere, they'd probably call me a fat bag."

Walt laughed and said, "And I'd be the old nag bag."

Carol said, "I could be the young bag."

Nina popped up and said,

> "Old bag, young bag,
> Fat bag, thin bag,
> Nag bag, sand bag,
> Boo!"

They laughed. Madden said, "I feel better already. Sometimes it's good to be silly. Stay awhile. I'll heat some soup."

Carol wondered whether they would. Aunt Madden did seem calmer, but it occurred to Carol her Aunt Madden was at loose ends. Depressed, maybe. "You only have two or three more weeks before you can go back to work, Aunt Madden," Carol said. "That's not a long time. Meanwhile you can watch me turn into a butterfly. I'm going to be sixteen in April, you know."

"Oh, you beautiful butterfly," Aunt Madden said, stretching out her arms to give her a hug. Carol felt her thin bony arms and shoulders and it made her sad. But, she was glad her Aunt smelled like she always did, something spicy and light and good. Something that reminded her of vanilla or lemon. That was her Aunt Madden Kendrick Boyer! A wonderful, wonderful person, not too strong, but a real fighter.

"I'll help you with the soup," Carol said.

Later that afternoon, Carol asked her mother, "What's the matter with Aunt Madden? She seems so wound up. Can't she relax now that she's almost over her breakdown?"

"She's scared, honey."

"Scared? Why? She's got us. She's got a nice place to live. She gets to travel."

"Sit down, Carol. I may as well tell you."

"What?"

"Aunt Madden is not well."

"I know that, mother."

"She's got cancer." Millie began to cry.

"Oh, mother, when did you know?" Carol stammered.

"The other night. She called. She didn't want to tell me. She said she wouldn't and couldn't. But she did."

"Why didn't you tell us?"

"She didn't want me to. She said she was going to handle this alone."

66

"But that's silly, mother. We're family."

"I know."

"Oh, mother," Carol said. "is there any hope?"

"Well, yes. We hope so. We think so. Surgery and all."

"I don't think I could live without Aunt Madden," Carol said looking at her hands. She was glad her mother reached over and put her arm around her.

"Mother, do other people have as many things going on in their families as we do in ours?"

"I think so. We just don't know about people sometimes. I think a lot of people are hurting. There's a lot of sorrow and pressure. Maybe more so in this day and age than before. No close ties—family and friends spread out all over the country. So, people bottle up their feelings, their hurts and troubles."

"Do you, mother?"

"Yes, sometimes," her mother said simply. "And you will too. Lots of times. Sometimes you'll think your hurt is unbearable. And then something or somebody will come along and you'll realize how fortunate you are."

"In spite of?"

"In spite of everything."

"Mother, I'm glad I can talk to you and dad about things. Do you know some of my friends never talk to their parents about the way they feel?"

"I know."

"Mother, I just feel terrible about Aunt Madden."

"Me too, honey." Millie got up and looked for a glass. "I'm thirsty. I think I'll have a glass of water."

"I'll get it for you," Carol said. She stood at the sink and turned on the faucet. Glancing out the window, she was amazed at what she saw! "Mother," she exclaimed, "come here! Look at the flood plain!"

They looked at the vast lake that had formed below them. Only a few spots of land here and there among the trees were poking out, big white humps of ice. The rest looked like a huge swamp. Mary Tree's Aunt Tildy had said Florida was one big swamp. Carol wondered if it looked like this!

It's like living on a lake, Carol thought. "I wonder if Nina's seen this," she said aloud.

Maybe she should call Reba. Then, an appalling thought occurred to her. If Reba had water in her basement when the water wasn't nearly so high, what would be happening now? Carol felt confused. There were so many things to worry about. Aunt Madden, Reba, the rumor about Nina she'd probably have to face at school, her English paper grade, and of course, getting to go to Disney World with Mary Tree. Always somebody or something to worry about. She stared out the window at the water. She'd seen water in the flood plain many times, but this was spooky. What if it rose higher? She was glad her house was on a bluff. Across the valley, the trees and limbs snapped around in the wind, their trunks and bases standing in cold swirling water. The sun was gone. Low gray clouds hung menacingly. Carol felt overwhelmed.

I'm only fifteen, she thought. *Why do I have so much to worry about?*

"Carol," Nina called downstairs.

"Yeah, what do you want?"

"Reba called you earlier."

"Why didn't you tell me?"

"She said to give you a message."

"What message?" Carol asked irritably.

"She wants to know if she can stay with us if she has to be evacuated—instead of going to her aunt's house."

"Well, I guess so. Why?"

"She didn't want to miss school. Her uncle and aunt live beyond Thomas Park. The school bus won't be able to pick up the kids from over there tomorrow because of the water. The roads are closed."

"Well, sure. If mom says it's okay." Carol didn't really mind. *I'll just have to tell her to cut out all the garbage each time she starts telling me how great I am. Why does she have to act like I'm so fantastic?* Carol wondered. *Always telling me I'm so smart, pretty, and creative. How disgusting. On the other hand, of course, I am all those things,* she admitted to herself, *but couldn't Reba just pipe it?* Everyone liked Reba in a way, and it was good to have Reba around saying nice things about her, especially when Eldon or Janice or Mary Tree or even Dick Moore could hear. *Poor Reba. She really should get with it,* Carol thought.

"Sure, sure. Tell Reba it's okay, Nina," she said.

"Aren't you going to call her?"

"No, you can tell her."

"Okay."

"Nina, did you know about Aunt Madden? She's got cancer."

"Cancer?" Nina's eyes widened with surprise.

"Yeah, mom told me. It's the kind you can operate on, though. She said Aunt Madden is scared."

"I'd be scared too."

"Me too," Carol said.

"Carol, Reba is scared too. She told me."

"Why? 'Cause she's got water in her basement?"

"No, it's more than that. It's their whole house. All her stuff. Everything."

"Her stuff isn't worth much, anyway," Carol said evenly.

"That's awful, Carol. How can you talk that way?"

"Well, it isn't. You know how things are at her place."

"But Carol, they are her things. What if they were yours?"

"I'd let all my junk wash away and then I could start over."

"Carol, you're awful!"

"Oh, Nina, I don't know why I'm saying that. I don't really. I just feel mean. I don't know why. Reba annoys me sometimes."

"You never told me that before."

"Why should I tell you something like that?"

"Well, I always thought you liked Reba. I'll tell her she can't come."

"No, you won't. I do and I don't like Reba. At least I'm honest about it. That's more than some people are."

"You're a rat!" Nina stormed. "I'm telling her she can come if mom says she can, and she can stay on my side of the room!" Nina slammed the door.

I am a rat, Carol thought. *A dirty, miserable rat in a dirty miserable world where people starve, get cancer, gossip, spread rumors, tell lies, are unemployed and suffer and get evacuated because of dumb floods!*

Chapter 7

REBA lay in bed thinking. She was on Nina's bed, and Nina was in a sleeping bag downstairs. Reba wondered what was happening to her father. He always scared her half to death when he yelled, and today he'd yelled at her about everything.

When she'd told him she was going to spend the night at Carol Norton's house, he'd yelled at her about staying home to help her mom. Her mom yelled, too. Reba knew it was good to let off steam, but her parents were ridiculous. Did Carol know, she wondered, how lucky it was to have parents who could talk? If her dad said the spaghetti sauce wasn't right or the potatoes were lumpy or the room was in a mess, her mom would yell at him and tell him to go fly a kite or go sit on a stump or a thousand other awful things. *I guess they get along,* she thought, *because they stay together, but they never talk! Just bicker, argue, fight, and yell. I wouldn't even care if they argued,* she thought, *if they just wouldn't yell!* It seemed Reba always searched for a quiet calmness. Carol Norton seemed to have it. Dick Moore seemed to have it. Mary Tree didn't—she was always nervously flitting back and forth. Janice didn't—she seemed too much on edge, a steely brittle kind of edge, something Reba could hardly put her finger on.

Reba sighed. How she loved it here, in this large quiet room. It was peaceful. She could hear Carol's breathing, the refrigerator humming, the furnace coming on. They were wonderful sounds! She turned over, fixed her pillow, and thought again about her parents. She was tired. Sleep would be good now, even if her house floated away. Her father was probably still standing on the basement steps yelling at her mother to bring buckets or pans to save the basement. Her mother was probably scurrying around, running back and forth yelling, "If you want this old place saved, do something yourself! Do you think I'm your slave?" Then she'd probably get the bucket and fling it at him. Reba fell asleep on the firm bed, like a feather coming softly to rest on the ground.

o   o   o

Early Monday morning, Carol awoke, turned, and reached for her earphones. Another school day unless they canceled school. But why should school be canceled? She almost smiled. It had become a habit each morning to find out while still in bed whether there would be school. She practically kept her radio at WOWO these days.

"And today," Bob Sievers was saying, "there will be no school in Allen County because of severe flooding." He listed another school district and Carol listened. When it came to her district, she heard that one of the schools would be closed because of boiler problems. Otherwise all schools

72

would be in session but buses would not be traveling over certain roads.

"Rats, school again." Secretly she was glad because of the many snow days they's already had. She really did get bored with all the confusion. Besides, her class was behind in so many subjects.

She groaned, stretched, and slipped out of bed. "Reba, get up. Wake up. We've got school today."

Reba shifted in her bed and turned. "Okay, okay. I'm getting up." They hurried, saying little as they dressed. Breakfast was almost ready, and they could hear Mrs. Norton downstairs. "Come on, Nina. Let's not be late today."

"Okay, mom. But, do I *have* to eat this stuff? I hate hot cereal. Other kids get all sorts of dry cereals, and I have to eat cream of wheat or oatmeal."

"What's the matter with you?" her mother was saying. "Just because your friends don't get up and eat a decent breakfast, you think it's the thing to do?"

"No, mom, I just don't like hot cereal. I like cornflakes and things."

"But, Nina, you get that from time to time, and you don't have to be picky about it." Millie Norton was firm.

"Well, I haven't had hot oatmeal in ages," Reba said. "I'd love some. Raisins in it, too! Oh, boy."

Carol looked at her. "Oh, come on. You've had that lots of times, I'll bet."

"Yeah, some of the time, but when I get it, mom yells at me about getting up and fixing it myself." Reba slipped her napkin into her lap and looked at Carol. "You don't know how lucky you are," she said almost in a whisper.

Millie Norton smiled but said nothing. Millie knew Carol had mixed feelings about Reba, but she herself liked Reba.

She knew her home was somehow special to Reba and it made her glad.

The girls hurried for the door, Nina tagging along. "I wish she'd walk faster," Carol said. "She just seems to forget there's such a thing as time."

Reba playfully tugged at Nina's scarf. "Come on, kid, let's go."

Carol wondered how Reba could be so patient with Nina. *Bet if she had a kid sister, she'd hate it,* she thought. Anyway, at least they were on their way.

Water gushed down the edges of the street into the rain sewers. It was a drab, dreary looking day and the trees moved their sticklike limbs against an even drearier grayer looking sky.

As the girls reached the corner where Nina left them, heading toward the elementary school, Carol remembered Marcia Compton. She turned back and called to Nina. When Nina was close enough so Reba couldn't hear, Carol said, "If I have a chance to bop Marcia, you can bet I'll do it. If anybody says anything, just ignore it."

Nina smiled gratefully. "Thanks." She waved and went on her way. Reba and Carol barely had time to catch the bus.

As they entered, they had to split up because the bus was crowded. "Sit here, Carol," Dick called.

"No thanks. I'm okay." Carol didn't want to sit with Dick. She not only would have to listen to his talk about himself but also worry about whether Reba would feel slighted. It would be easier if she just didn't sit with him. Reba, she noticed, was sitting down next to Marcia Compton.

Carol turned around and said to Marcia, "I'd like to talk with you when we get off."

"Okay," Marcia said flippantly and continued to talk to

74

Reba. Carol felt herself getting angry. If Marcia Compton started anything about Nina, she'd really be in for it. The bus stopped suddenly.

"Why? What? What's the matter?" Dick asked for all of them.

"Too much water here," the bus driver said. "I don't want to go through this. I'd better turn around here."

"You should hear what's happening in Fort Wayne," Reba said to Dick.

"Don't tell me. I already know firsthand," he answered. "The rivers are rising so fast, they're really worried and some sandbagging has started down there. There's a lot of flooding and there's a lot of evacuation going on. You should see how high the rivers are!"

"We've got water in our basement," Reba said. "What about you, Dick?"

"It's bad," Dick answered. "There's water in the street and the yard, but so far there's nothing in our house." He sounded concerned. Carol was surprised. She'd no idea the water was spreading so much. The flood plain was like a river outside her house, but she began to wonder whether it would rise as high as their deck.

"Dick," she asked, "how much more water do you think we'll get? It looks like an ocean behind our house." She laughed.

Dick shrugged his shoulders. He didn't laugh. "Don't know. A couple of feet, maybe."

"Then the water may get in the old groundhog's hole," Carol said.

"Your mom and dad wouldn't care about that, would they?" Reba said. "Maybe they'd move away and your mom could have her garden."

They talked about groundhogs, the water, the problems

75

of using the First or Seventh Street bridges, and before they knew it, the bus was at school. Carol got off before Reba and Marcia. Dick went striding on ahead.

Marcia waited at the edge of the steps.

"Nina told me what happened on Friday," Carol began.

"I didn't say she *stole* the money," Marcia answered. "I just said she *had* the money."

"You're a rat. Why did you make her stand there and apologize and let Mr. Cranston think she took it? And how did Mr. Cranston know she had it? You must have called or something. You, you. . . ." Carol was so angry she couldn't think of an awful enough word to use.

"I'm sorry."

"Sorry? Is that all you can say? You accuse my sister of stealing and all you can say is you're sorry?"

"I—I—I . . . well, I don't know, I just did it."

"You just did it? What did Nina ever do to you to make you want to hurt her like that? Besides, how in the world did you know she had your money? You were already on the bus!" Carol was indignant. "Who did your dirty work?"

Marcia hung her head. "I'm sorry. Jamie Batonet saw the money blow out of my pocket, and he told me after I got on the bus that Nina picked it up."

"She wasn't going to keep it."

"Well. . . ."

"Well, how did you get Mr. Cranston and Mrs. Doonsberger in on it?" Carol demanded, her fists clinched.

"I thought about it all day. It—it . . . was a dirty trick and I'm sorry."

"Sorry?"

"Yeah, I'm sorry. I called Mr. Cranston before noon and told him I'd lost my money and that somebody told me Nina Norton had taken it. I am sorry."

"That's not enough, Marcia. Nina felt awful. What if it got around school that Nina Norton had done such an awful thing? What does Mr. Cranston think now? Can you imagine what he must think about the Nortons? How do you think you'd feel if Mr. Cranston thought you were a thief? Nina can hardly look at him!"

Marcia nodded and twisted her hands around her books. The wind whipped her hair back, and her nose was red because of the cold. "I really am sorry, Carol."

"Why did you do it?"

"Because—oh, I don't know. Nina just gets everything I want, I guess."

"Like being picked to be the Booth Girl at the Carnival?"

"Well...."

"Well, that's just tough luck! You're going to tell Nina you're sorry! You're going to tell Mr. Cranston and Mrs. Doonsberger the truth! You're going to apologize to Nina, and you're going to tell Jamie Batonet that Nina didn't take your money, and...." Carol caught her breath, "and if you don't I'm personally going to spread it all over school what you did to Nina! And—and I'm going to tell them some other stuff too!"

"Like what?"

"Like you're an envious little prig!"

"Oh, Carol, I said I'm sorry. And I am not a prig. That's an awful word."

"Not as bad as the word 'thief' and you know it!"

"Like I said, Carol, I'm sorry. I'll tell Mr. Cranston how it happened."

"Well, we'll see. I'll talk to Nina this afternoon and if you haven't, you'll be in for some real trouble!"

The bell rang, so Carol gave Marcia a hard look and said, "You'll see." She strode off.

Marcia turned and ran toward the middle school building. Inside the long hall, Carol noticed crowds of students milling about. There was excitement in the air.

Reba came up to Carol. "Get it straightened out?"

"How did you know?"

"Nina told me last night. And," Reba continued, "on the bus today Marcia said she had a feeling you were going to jump all over her. She admitted she'd done an awful thing to Nina and felt just terrible about it."

"What else did she say?"

"She said she couldn't sleep last night because she knew she'd done wrong. She knew she had it coming. She planned to talk to Mr. Cranston today."

"Well, I'm glad," Carol said. "She should."

"You were really fighting for Nina, weren't you?" Reba asked.

Carol nodded. As they went into home room, Carol said, "I guess so. She drives me crazy sometimes, but Nina wouldn't harm a flea. Trouble with her is she doesn't have the spunk to fight back. You know, stand up for herself. She'll learn though."

"She doesn't like to fight," Reba whispered. "Neither do I. I think I understand how she feels."

Carol hurried over to sharpen her pencil. *Reba would never understand how Nina is,* she thought. *Reba is too interested in pleasing everybody.*

"Reba," Mrs. Atlee said, "you're wanted in the office immediately."

Reba's face turned pale. Reba looked at Carol, and Carol saw the look of fear that crossed her face.

Chapter 8

CAROL didn't see Reba the rest of the day. On the way home, she sat across from Dick on the bus and asked him about Reba.

"Her house," Dick said. "It's flooded. The basement is full, and the whole first floor is under water, or so I hear."

"My goodness! You mean there's water right in the living room and the kitchen and all?" Carol could hardly believe such a thing.

"I'm scared to go home myself," said Dick. "The water keeps getting closer. If it gets any worse, I don't know what we'll do. Dad's talking about more sandbags. I think we're going to try to wrap the bottom part of the house in plastic and pile bags around that."

"Is that possible?" Carol couldn't imagine.

"When it gets bad, you'll do anything."

"I guess I never really thought it would get this bad," Carol said sympathetically.

"Reba's house is in a low spot. I think they're ruined." Dick sounded upset.

"Well, yes, I guess so," Carol said. Somehow in spite of the fact that Reba always seemed to be around, Carol had never really given much thought to Reba as a person. No one probably cared. Reba was drab and plain, really. Her folks always argued. Carol wondered how Reba felt. She realized she'd never gotten to know Reba, the real Reba. Suddenly it seemed important to find out how Reba was. She looked out at the muddy ground. *Water, water everywhere,* she thought miserably. And it looked like more rain any minute.

"Mom, is Nina home?" Carol called.

"I'm here," Nina answered. "Mom went to the church."

"Why? Today's Monday."

"They've set up a Flood Relief Committee."

"Really? What will they do?"

"Mom said they'd do anything and everything— whatever had to be done. Find places for people who are being evacuated, provide food. Lots of things."

"I'm going to call Reba. She went home today from school."

"You won't get her," Nina said. "Her house is flooded out. They evacuated everybody in that block late last night, or at least that's what Mr. Cranston said."

"Mr. Cranston? That reminds me, Nina. Did he talk to you? Did Marcia Compton?"

"Yes. Mr. Cranston called me to the office at nine o'clock. I was scared to death."

"What did he say?"

"He apologized. He admitted he'd been too hasty on Friday and asked me to forgive him. He said he should have let me explain."

80

"Well, he should have!"

"He never really accused me," Nina said. "He just asked if I had the money. I was too scared to talk."

"And Marcia?"

"She's sorry. She called me this afternoon. I think she felt really bad."

"I hope you told her off. Did you?"

"No."

"You didn't?"

"I didn't need to. I couldn't have. She started crying and told me I'd probably hate her for the rest of my life."

"Yeah?"

"I told her to forget it. It was okay."

"How could you do that, Nina? She should have gotten it from you!"

"I don't know, Carol. I think she was sorry. Mom said that's the worse kind of punishment, but I never really thought so. But after talking with Marcia today, I think maybe mom's right."

"Well, it's up to you. I talked to Marcia this morning. I hope she remembers what I said. Anyway, I'm glad it's over. I don't think I'd be able to forgive and forget so easily."

Carol looked at Nina and shook her head. "You're different, but as a sister, I guess you'll do."

Nina laughed. "Want a peanut butter sandwich?"

"Yeah, I'm starved."

"Guess what we're doing tomorrow," Nina said, watching Carol spread a big goop of jelly on her bread. "We have to go to school from 12:30 to 4:40 in the afternoon."

"Why?"

"Because the basement is flooded at McIntosh School, and those kids have to use our school until they get their furnace fixed."

"You mean they go in the morning to Auburn Elementary? And then you go in the afternoon? Huh, that's a switch."

"There's water all over the playground at school," Nina continued. "We call it the Atlantic Ocean."

"Yeah, there's water all over northeast Indiana right now. How's the creek, I wonder?" Carol jumped up to look at the flood plain. Water had come high on the bluff and spread like a sheet across through the trees to the far side where water spilled from the creek. It no longer resembled a swamp. "You can't see the creek," Carol cried. "It's solid water!"

At supper that night Millie Norton said Walt wouldn't be home. "He's helping sandbag the Messenger Corporation. They're going to work through the night."

"Mom, it's getting bad, isn't it? Reba's house is washed out," Carol said.

"Reba's house has water in it up to the top of the kitchen counter. They are hard hit," Millie answered.

"Where is Reba now? I tried to phone her, but nobody answers."

"With her relatives. Her dad is crushed. Her mother just sits and cries. Everything they had is gone."

"And what about Reba?" Carol asked again.

"She's with them."

"Mom," Carol said, "could Reba move in with us for a while? She could wear some of my things."

Millie put a spoon in the tuna fish casserole and dished some out on their plates. She was tired but happy.

"I'd love that, Carol. That's sweet. Would you like to go with me to get her?"

"Yes. Right now."

"In about an hour. The church took some food over there,

so we'll scoot over when we finish. That house where they're staying isn't big, and her aunt has taken in some other neighbors besides."

"Oh, mother, I can't wait." Carol felt Nina looking at her, so she retorted, "What's the matter with you?"

"Nothing, I just thought Reba bothered you a lot."

"She's still a friend. Even if she does bother me sometimes. I have a heart, you know."

"You girls are kind," Millie said. "Even if sometimes I wouldn't know it." She laughed at them but reached over and squeezed Carol's hand.

"You do have a heart, honey. It's just that sometimes you don't let yourself show it. But I know."

Carol thought about what her mother said. She seemed to have so many conflicting feelings. Sometimes she felt good and kind and clean and confident. She could beat the world. But sometimes she felt hateful. Knock anybody down who got in her way. Hate them all and not feel one ounce of pity for anybody or anything . . . not even a dying dog, as Nina accused her one time. Funny thing about that dog, though, she'd cried later when no one had known. Hardhearted? She wasn't hardhearted. It was just easier for her that way. What did Nina know? For that matter what did anyone really know about her?

"Pass the butter, mom." Carol was hungry, and thinking made her tired.

It wasn't long before they picked up Reba. She was sitting in a chair in the small house holding a suitcase on her lap. When she saw Carol, she jumped up and cried, "Oh, Carol! I'm so glad you're here."

Carol hugged Reba. The other people in the room never seemed to notice. They continued talking with each other. Some were standing around. Others stared out the window, pointing in the direction of the creek. There was a warm comfortable feeling of belonging.

"Where are your folks?" Carol asked, reaching for Reba's bag.

"Dad's down at the house still, I think," Reba said. "He says everything he ever worked for is lost."

"He's got the house, doesn't he?" Carol asked. "That's something."

"The house? What house? We don't have enough money to fix it. Dad's been laid off from his job since last September. I don't know. We'll knuckle down somehow. Either that, or call it quits."

"Come on. You're going to stay with us," Carol said. "Do you have anything else? Records? Books?"

"No. Nothing, right now. We've a few things packed in some boxes, but they are in my uncle's garage."

The impact of Reba's situation hit Carol. "You mean this is *all* you have?"

"Yes, only this suitcase." Reba tried to look brave, but tears began sliding down her face. She turned toward the window.

"Oh, Reba, come on." Carol led her gently outside. "Go ahead and cry. You must feel terrible." Carol looked at Reba and instead of steeling herself against the hurt she saw in her friend's face, she too began to cry.

There they stood on the top step, crying and hugging each other. In the car, Millie reached for Nina's hand.

"Your uncaring sister, our 'hardhearted Hannah,' as you call her, isn't really that way, is she?"

"No, mom. Not really. But she seemed to change that summer our dog got killed, remember? Just when she finished middle school. We used to swing and play and run and laugh. What happened?"

"Nothing, Nina. She's just growing up. She's got a lot of feelings to sort out."

"Will she? Ever?"

"No one ever gets everything sorted out. You learn to deal with life as it comes. Do the best you can and keep-a-going. It's hard, especially if you try to do it alone." She flicked on the radio. An announcer was speaking, ". . . and people from all over Fort Wayne and surrounding communities are volunteering. If you can help sandbag, just come to the coliseum, the back entrance, and they'll tell you what to do."

"Mom," Carol said as she got in the car, "most of Reba's things are gone. She'll have to borrow my clothes. She's my size, though. It'll be no problem."

"I'm glad about that," Reba said. "And I'm glad I'm going to your house."

Millie smiled. "I've always needed another daughter, Reba. Your mom will just have to share you with me."

"Mom's really upset. She's talking about going back to New Jersey. She thinks her family would take her in. Didn't know about dad, though. She said he could stay out here if he wanted."

"Don't worry about all that now, Reba. Your mother is probably in a state of shock. It will take her time to sort things out."

"Last I heard," Reba said, "dad was in a boat at the house yelling at the water." She tried to laugh.

There was nothing Carol nor her mother could say.

That night sitting crosslegged on Carol's bed, Reba told Carol and Nina about the flood. "My dad tried to do everything. Nothing worked. Do you know," she said to Nina, "water was actually flowing right across our kitchen counter!"

Nina's eyes were wide.

"The door was open, and they, the Civil Defense, took a canoe and paddled right through the living room into the downstairs bedroom!"

"You mean paddled through your house? Like it was a river or something?" Nina asked incredulously.

They talked for a long time. "I didn't know it was so bad," Carol said. "I mean you can look out the window here and see the flood plain and it looks like a huge lake, but somehow you don't worry about it too much."

"Yeah, yesterday I saw two mallards out there," Nina said. "Can you believe that? Just like it was a duck pond or something."

"The radio says it's terrible in Fort Wayne. They're working on the dikes down there. Trying to keep them shored up. Volunteers have been working all night. Dad's down at the Messenger Corporation helping them."

"It's awful. Somehow it doesn't seem like it can get worse, but it does," Reba said. "The rivers haven't stopped rising yet."

"It's supposed to rain tomorrow," Nina said. "I heard that over TV tonight."

"Oh, no! Not rain?" the girls questioned.

"That's scary." They jumped up to look out the window, but it was dark, and they could see nothing but the glimmer of lights from the downstairs reflecting on the water.

"You girls have to get to bed," Millie said, coming into their room. "You've got school tomorrow, believe it or not."

"But I don't have to get up early," Nina said. "Remember I go to school in the afternoon."

"You're lucky. Everything is so different now." Carol shrugged. "School schedules changed. People moving. I don't know, everybody and everything seems different."

"They are different," Reba said. "You wouldn't believe how people are helping out, bringing food, clothes, working to help each other, even for people they don't know. It's amazing."

"It's an emergency, isn't it, mom?" Nina asked.

"It really is, honey. And in Fort Wayne, it's a disaster."

As Carol lay in bed that night, it occurred to her she hadn't thought about Mary Tree nor Disney World all day. But then, she realized with a start, she hadn't thought about her Aunt Madden either.

She slipped quietly downstairs. She saw her mother standing at the patio door overlooking the flood plain, an expressionless look on her face.

Was her mother worried? Frightened? Was the water rising? She didn't know.

She came near her mother and quietly asked, "Mother, what's wrong?"

Chapter 9

"YOUR FATHER isn't home yet," Carol's mother said. "They're trying to save as much as possible down by the Messenger Corporation. I just listened to the eleven o'clock news, and in Fort Wayne the dikes aren't holding. The rivers are still rising. They don't expect them to crest until Wednesday or Thursday."

"It's supposed to rain tomorrow," Carol said.

"I know. Let's hope it doesn't."

"Mom, how is it with Aunt Madden?"

"Her house is fine. She says she's going with me in the morning to work with the flood relief people at the church."

"What about her, though?"

"It's not too bad, she thinks. We talked about it again this morning, and the doctors think a simple operation will remove the cancer. But you know Aunt Madden. She worries herself almost to death sometimes. She's got to get involved doing something."

"There's plenty she can do with all this flooding, isn't there?"

"You're right. But I don't know that she will. All this confusion might make her too nervous. She shouldn't have too much stress right now."

"She seems just the opposite of you in so many ways, mom."

"Well, she is in some ways but not in others. Most people are about the same when it comes to important things. But I do think Madden is on the verge of settling down. She'd like to take life as it comes. She's always had this feeling that life would pass her by if she didn't tack it down first. And then Uncle Ben."

"Is that why she's always going off on trips since Uncle Ben died?"

"Yes, I think that's part of it. He died when you were ten—a heart attack, remember? She's been so nervous ever since."

"Sometimes I can almost remember Uncle Ben," Carol said. "He was big and strong, wasn't he?"

"He was. And he was good, too," Millie said.

"Aunt Madden can be strong, too," Carol said. "She's a fighter, a survivor."

"Shouldn't you be in bed? When did you start doing such heavy thinking anyway?" Millie looked at Carol and smiled.

"Mom, everything is changing. Every day something makes me feel a different way. Am I going crazy or something?"

"You're growing up, honey. And when you're way over forty, you'll find things keep changing. The more they change, the more they stay the same."

"That doesn't make sense."

"I mean the more things change around us, the more we

realize the only things that are important are family, love, being true to oneself, and friendship. That sort of thing."

"The tie that binds, huh?"

"The tie that binds," her mother agreed. "Now go to bed." Carol hugged her mother. Things would work out. Somehow she knew they would.

The next day again there was school. Many schools were closed, but not Carol's. Not yet. Some schools were excusing students, if they had notes from parents, to help with the sandbagging in Fort Wayne. Announcers kept asking for more help. Many parts of Fort Wayne were evacuated. Dikes were beginning to sag. The mayor was interviewed after surveying the damage. He told reporters it would cost the city thousands and thousands of dollars. The problems, damage, and costs to many homeowners were staggering.

On the way to school, Reba and Carol asked Dick about his house.

"I think we'll be okay," he said cautiously. "I wanted to stay home, but dad told me I'd be better off at school. If they still need volunteers tomorrow in Fort Wayne, dad said I could go. I think a group from school is going."

"You mean from our school?" Reba was interested.

"Yes. Dad talked to the high school principal yesterday, and I think they're planning to take a busload down to help."

"Wonder if we can go?" Carol and Reba asked.

"Might as well help somebody else," Reba said. "My house, well, it's too late for us."

Dick promised he'd let them know about the volunteer group as they hurried to get to their rooms before the bell.

The students could talk of nothing else but the flood. Clouds hung low and dark, but still no rain fell. Everyone went around talking about rain. Everyone wondered if the dikes would hold. In just a few days, everything in northeast Indiana had changed. People had changed, attitudes changed, the weather kept changing, and there was anticipation in the air that spoke of fear, frustration, hope, desperation, and determination.

"It's like surviving," Carol said to Reba. "It's like there's nothing else. We go on with our classes, our chores, and all, but they aren't important."

"Surviving the flood. That's all that counts," Reba agreed.

All the way to and from school, they saw signs of flooding. Streets were closed, cars parked in unusual places, canoes pulled up in suburban yards, and it was hard to find any dry places to walk. The sky seemed to get grayer and darker by the minute. The wind blew, and a raw coldness made it no longer possible to wear just jackets.

Behind the Norton house the flood plain spread as far as the creek and beyond. Brackish debris floated and swirled. Nina saw an old white football flowing in the current, just four feet from their back steps. "That water isn't standing still," Nina said. "It's moving!"

"The wind whips it around," Carol said.

"No, no," her mother corrected. "Watch carefully. There's a strong current there. You can see it if you look closely. Watch that pile of trash. See how it's moving."

The girls stood by the back door staring at the water. Wind snapped the trees and the dark sky looked as though it would pour buckets and buckets of water in just seconds.

"There are those mallards again!" Nina exclaimed.

The girls were fascinated. Paddling around as happy as ducks can be were two mallards. One was a good-looking male, the other, the female, drab and brown, practically blending with the water and underbrush.

"I'm seeing things I've never seen out here before," Carol told Reba. "We have our groundhogs, of course, but we've seen an opossum, ducks, strange birds."

"Yes, and I smelled a skunk last night," Nina said. "I think the animals are moving to higher ground."

"If there are any left, you mean," Reba said.

Carol pointed to the ground hog burrow. "Oh, no," she wailed. "Mom, look at this. The groundhog hasn't left. He's just made another opening two or three inches higher than his old one!"

They looked and sure enough, his cavelike opening with the sandy porch was now awash in water, but neatly above it, was a new hole.

"What an engineer!" Millie said. "I give up. I'll never have a garden if this keeps up!"

The telephone rang and Carol went to answer it.

"Mother," she said, coming back shortly, "Dick and the senior highs from church are going to Fort Wayne on Thursday to help sandbag. Can we go? Our minister is going. They're taking a van. Some other kids are going from school in a bus."

Millie hesitated. She wasn't quite sure about letting her girls go.

"Mother, please," Carol begged. "The schools are excusing people who have notes from their parents. They need extra help down there."

"Mrs. Norton, please let us go," Reba said. "Look at my house. It's ruined. Maybe we can help save somebody else's place."

Millie nodded. "There's so much you can do here in our little town."

"But the group is going, and mother, please...."

"If your dad says it's okay, I'll let you go." Millie looked at them squarely. "Stay with your group. Follow directions. Call me if . . . ."

"Oh, mother, you know we will!" Carol interrupted.

"Can I go?" Nina asked.

"No, honey. I can't let you go. You have school in the afternoon, and besides, I don't want you down there in that mob."

"Other kids are there. All kinds of people. I saw them on television—kids, teenagers, even little old ladies with blue hair."

"No, Nina." Her mother was firm.

"Aunt Madden said she thought she ought to go. She said she could borrow dad's waders," Nina said.

"She probably would go, if she could," Millie said. "Then it would be different, Nina."

The girls could hardly wait. "It'll be exciting," Carol said.

"Not just exciting," Reba said. "It's more than that. It's desperate."

"Well, yes," Carol acknowledged. "I guess so."

"Desperate and sad," Reba said. "Desperate and sad and exciting."

"What should we wear?" Carol looked at Reba.

"Raincoats, boots, warm clothes," her mother answered. "It will be cold."

"Guess what?" Nina said. "This boy in school said when his family was evacuated, they had to leave behind their cat and dog."

"That's terrible. What happened to them?" Reba asked.

"They called the humane shelter and asked them to save the animals."

"Did they?" Carol asked.

"I don't know," Nina said. "Our teacher said lots of animals are being deserted. Some have drowned."

"Oh, that's awful," Millie said.

"Our teacher said the humane shelter needs more volunteers."

"I hadn't even thought of that," Carol said. "Maybe we should volunteer."

"You'd have to have a canoe," Nina said disparagingly. "You'd have to paddle right through houses and barns."

"Just imagine how great you'd feel if you saved someone's pet," Carol said.

"You girls better hurry up and get to bed," Millie said. "I'm going to call Madden. I want to hear more about her visit to the doctor today. Nina, go get your sleeping bag ready."

The girls went upstairs. It wasn't long before Nina was settled. But Reba and Carol weren't sleepy. They listened to the radio. "Rain should fall sometime in the night. Two more inches are expected," an announcer said. The girls groaned.

The mayor of Fort Wayne came on and appealed to every person to help with the sandbagging. The girls could hardly believe it when they heard the emergency operations center had called for the evacuation of 9,000 more homes. "Thousands of volunteers are shoveling sand into bags. Some twenty thousand bags an hour, but there is still a desperate need for more volunteers," the announcer said. He explained that the student council president of North Side High School had appealed to all area students to come out and help. "From Spy Run to the east side at Pemberton Road, the news is depressing. David J. Kiester, in charge of Fort Wayne's volunteer flood-fighters, says that if you've only an hour or so to help, that's okay. Come on out to the Coliseum and help. Mayor Win Moses describes Pemberton Dike as being as soggy as toothpaste, and Carl O'Neil, city transportation director, says the five-block-long retaining wall down at Pemberton is holding back a swell of water some ten feet deep and at least two miles long. If that breaks, some three square miles of homes will be washed away.

"The mayor is trying to get this area of northeast Indiana declared a disaster area so we can get some federal aid," the announcer continued.

Reba shrugged. "I don't know what to say. I hope they make it. At least we'll be helping tomorrow."

"I hope it won't be too late," Carol said. "It sounds awful." They listened some more. "This is certainly one of Fort Wayne's finest hours," an announcer said. "Students and volunteers are coming from everywhere. No matter what happens, it's a wonderful thing the way people are helping each other. People will have stories to tell about this for years. By the way, we've got some callers here who'd like to relate some experiences they've had. Here's a lady. Let's listen to her story."

The woman said, "For two days my little dog, Fluffy, kept running around and around the house, like he was spooked or something. We tried to settle him down, tried to feed him. No use. He just wouldn't settle down. He'd take his little bowl and run around trying to find some place to put it. He kept this up for two days. We never saw anything like it. He just wouldn't be satisfied. It was like he was frantic or something. He'd never done such a thing before. He must have sensed something. Two days later when we had to evacuate, we realized he'd been trying to tell us something."

Reba and Carol looked at each other. "Do you suppose animals really know?" Carol asked.

"Dad says they do," Reba answered.

"Dad had a cat named Oreo one time, who thought he was a dog," Carol said. "The cat came when he whistled, walked alongside him, acted just like a dog."

"Sounds like a dog," Reba laughed. "I once had a goat. We lived in the country then, and I had a little goat." Reba smiled ruefully. "We sold him when we moved to town."

"I didn't know you lived in the country," Carol said.

"Oh, yes, when dad still had his business. He had a feed and seed store. It wasn't big, but it was big enough. It kept him happy, I guess. At least he seemed happy then."

"Why did he sell it? Where was it?"

"It was on the south side of town. He sold out when the Milligan Brothers put in that big plant."

"Did somebody else take over the business?"

"Well, yes and no." Reba shrugged. "I guess some of the farm businesses took over the feed part. Grocery stores and discount stores sell seed now."

"Why doesn't he start a business again?" Carol asked. "You said he was out of work."

"Mom, I think. She used to say he should have a regular income, steady hours, you know, so we could be a regular family. Well, anyway, dad made good money at the factory. They had to cut back, though, and he didn't have much seniority. Then last September he was laid off. It's been almost seven months now."

"Is he going back soon? Does he receive unemployment?"

"The money ran out a couple of months ago."

Carol turned off the radio and listened.

"Dad gets down. He yells at mom, at me, the economy, everything. He says some pretty awful things about America, too," Reba said quietly.

"It's still a good place, one of the best," Carol said.

"Yeah, I know. He knows too, but he gets bitter. He says a man should be able to support his family. All that stuff."

"I'm really sorry," Carol said. "I had no idea you were having such a tough time. You should have told me."

"Oh, come on. You were pretty busy with your friends."

"What friends?"

"You know—Janice, Mary Tree, Dick."

"They're all my friends, sure, in a way. But none are close, really close," Carol said.

"But you're never alone," Reba said. "You're always in the middle of things. Sometimes I used to be afraid to speak to you because you seemed so busy with everybody else."

"You mean I didn't have time for you?" Carol asked. "You're silly." But as she straightened her pillow, she remembered guiltily how many times she'd been annoyed with Reba. Reba always standing around, wanting to belong, never quite sure of herself. Reba who never had much to say, who just seemed to tag along the edge of things. Really though, Reba was cute, with her black curly hair, brown eyes, and wide smile. She had a nice figure and could wear just about anything. But she should hold up her shoulders more. "You know," Carol said, "Aunt Madden said pretend there is a thread attached to the top of your head. Pretend someone is pulling you up by that single thread. It will make you stand tall."

Carol brushed her hair. She realized with a start she'd never heard anyone ask Reba for anything, not an opinion, not to spend the night, nothing. How could they not know how good it was to talk with Reba? Flexing her toes upward, she turned, grinned at Reba, and said, "Next time I act like I'm too busy or something, give me a punch. I'm not a hotshot, you know. You know how it is in school. 'Gotta act cool.'"

Reba laughed. "Dad says they used to say, 'Gotta be with it.'"

"Yeah, and my folks said they used to say 'hot stuff.'"

"Funny, from generation to generation, I guess people mean the same thing," Reba said.

"Let's forget being hot or cool or with it," Carol said. "Let's just be friends."

"You are a friend, Carol. I've never had a friend like you. It doesn't matter, does it, what you've got or what I've got? Just that we care about each other, right?"

"Yeah," Carol agreed.

"And that doesn't mean we shut other people out either," Reba added. "You know, Carol, you've done all these things for me. I haven't done anything for you. A friendship can't be one-sided, can it?"

"Don't be silly, Reba. Mom says a friendship is like a wave. It ebbs and flows. First you do something for me, then maybe I do something for you. Who counts? It evens out."

"Well, I hope I can do something for you someday. Introduce you to a millionaire, something." Reba laughed. "I'm tired, Carol. Let's get some sleep."

Chapter 10

"AUNT MADDEN almost decided to go," Nina said to Carol and Reba, as they dressed. "She called to wish you luck. Said if she were going, she'd wear dad's waders. You'd better wear good rubber boots."

"We're ready," Carol said, pulling on another sweater. "Last night they interviewed somebody who'd been working, and he said it was brutally cold."

"I'll worry about you," Millie said. "When it's wet like this, it can be awfully bitter out there. Don't leave your rain hats in the bus."

"We won't." The girls were excited, but a little nervous.

By eight o'clock, the group was on its way. Laughing, talking, their high jinks and jokes seemed almost unreal against the backdrop of disaster and dreariness outside.

Arriving in Fort Wayne, they joined a huge milling crowd that didn't seem to know where to go or what to do. Some people barked out orders, and somebody told them about a movie in the basement of the Coliseum which would show them how to sandbag. Somebody else was talking about getting sandwiches and coffee. Gradually Carol's group joined thousands of volunteers in the line. They passed sandbags from one to another.

Some volunteers from Berne were next to Reba and Carol, several Amish farmers beyond them, and down the line a bit were several patrolmen. Somebody began singing as the bags came moving down the line and the tune slinked along as the bags came swinging by.

"Catch it, Reba," Carol called.

"Got it."

"Here's another one."

"I've got it," Reba said laughing.

They threw them on and on and on, with exhilaration and camaraderie.

"Here, catch," Dick called to Carol.

"Got it."

"Here, Reba, pass it on."

"Okay."

The sky got grayer. It had drizzled off and on, but now it looked like it would pour.

"It'll be just our luck, if it rains," somebody called out.

"How are things down there?" another person asked.

"Let us in." A group of four got in line.

"Where're you from?" Reba asked, tossing a bag to the first boy.

"Angola."

"Oh, how are things there? Any flooding?"

"Not too much. Mostly in the fields and low spots."

"You should see our town," Carol called.

"My house, you mean," Reba said. "It's a disaster! Water all the way up to the kitchen counter!"

"Around the lake, in Steuben County," another boy said, "the water is above the docks and in a lot of cottages. My dad had a car parked in the yard and it's totally covered."

"The whole car?"

"Yeah, it's ruined."

"Why didn't he move it?" Dick asked.

"By the time we got there, the motor was flooded. We couldn't even pull it out."

"What about a boat?" Reba asked. "They took a boat right into my house!"

"We didn't have a boat there. It was in storage."

"It's a mess everywhere! The highway between Auburn and Hamilton is impassable," somebody else said as he joined the line.

"Where's this bag going?" Carol asked. "I mean where is it going *to* down the line?"

"Somebody told me they're packing them around somebody's house," Dick answered, "down near the river."

"No, no. It's a secondary sandbag dike they're building," a person from Butler said. "Our group just went to see."

"Look at all this water!" Reba exclaimed.

"I'd rather look at this than what's on the other side of the dike," a man said. "That levee has the consistency of toothpaste, at least that's the way the mayor put it. It's some fifteen feet above the level of the houses."

An Amish farmer agreed. "No use to do anything here if this dike goes. It would flood at least 10,000 people, maybe more."

"The mayor is supposed to come out here again to look things over," another person said.

"On TV they said he'd been here most of the night," another boy from Angola said.

"Where you from?" the Amish farmer asked.

"Tri State College. Angola. What about you?"

"We're from near Grabill," the Amishman answered.

"Nice to meet ya," the college boy said.

They grinned and tossed the sacks down the line.

"Sure looks like rain," an Amish teenager said.

"Any minute now," Reba agreed.

"Look, there's a reporter! A reporter and a camera!" somebody called.

"Oh, boy, maybe we'll be on television!"

"I don't know. Looks like they are taking pictures of the dike. Let's tell them to aim the camera this way," the group from near Berne said.

"What dike is this, anyway?" Carol asked.

"Pemberton. Pemberton Road dike," an Amishman said.

"Oh," Carol tossed another bag to Reba.

"This is just one bad place, too. You should see how it is over on Sherman Boulevard. This town has some 35 miles of dikes," somebody said tossing a sack.

Carol's arms ached. She realized she was tired, but she clinched her teeth and said, "I won't stop." Calling to Reba, she yelled, "Here, Reba, catch."

"Got it. Here you go." Reba tossed the bag of sand to the person next to her.

It began to spit rain. "Oh, no!" everyone moaned. "Rain."

The line rippled as they pulled hats and collars closer. But the bags kept coming and the sandbagging continued.

"How long you folks been here?" Reba asked the people from Berne.

"Since four or five this morning. We're knocking off around ten or eleven."

"You've been here since four this morning?" Carol was amazed.

"Yeah, we took over from a group from the Indiana

Purdue Regional campus. They came in before midnight."

"Midnight?"

"That's right. This line's been holding since last Sunday!"

Carol felt a surge of pride. She was part of an overall effort to save the city. She straightened her back and shook her head to spin off the rain from her hat. So far it hadn't poured, but if it did, she vowed she'd stand right there and sandbag.

"Do you know it's spring?"

"You mean almost spring, don't you?" Reba answered.

"Well, the groundhog is out, the snow is gone, and this morning on the radio on the *Little Red Barn* program, I heard Mr. Sievers say a man called him from Monroeville to tell him he'd found a snake in his backyard."

"That's spring! Who needs a calendar?" Dick said.

The Amish farmer overheard and said, "It may be spring but it sure feels like winter."

It was cold, a raw cold dampness that pierced to their very bones. But, the line kept moving sandbags.

"My arms ache," Reba said.

"My nose is dripping," Carol said.

"How long have we been here, anyway?" Dick asked after a time.

"Not long, maybe an hour or so?" Carol was guessing.

"Oh, no, at least more than that," Reba disagreed.

"Ask that man with a watch."

"Okay. Hey, what time is it?" Dick asked a man.

"Two fifteen."

"We've been here six hours! I can't believe this!" Carol was amazed.

"It seems like we just got here!" Dick said.

"Yeah, but I'm tired," Reba said. "My arms are tired. My whole body is tired."

For an instant, Carol felt a twinge of irritation. How could Reba or anyone admit to being tired? Didn't they realize how important they were? They were saving the city of Fort Wayne! She glanced around behind her. There were new crowds milling about, people joining the lines, others leaving. Suddenly Carol felt a huge sense of relief. She *was* tired, and she was grateful for the hundreds and hundreds of volunteers. All together, everybody working, they'd do it. They would save the city. She couldn't do it alone, but she had helped.

"I am tired," she admitted to Reba. "Really tired. Hungry, cold, and damp."

"Me too!" Reba agreed.

Just then Dick called, "Mr. Van Houston said we'd knock off soon."

"Who's Mr. Van Houston?" Reba asked.

"Here, catch!" Carol took a sandbag and passed it on. She was tired but exhilarated. She had done something. Maybe not much, but she had done something worthwhile and she felt good.

"Mr. Van Houston," Dick answered, "seems to be the person in charge here." Some other people pointed.

Carol saw a man talking with her minister.

"Fifteen more minutes, Carol," Reba said.

"Fifteen?" Carol shrugged. "Okay." It seemed like an eternity.

"There's chili coming. Chili or sandwiches. Which do you want?"

"A sandwich, I guess. Anything."

"Don't go for the sandwiches," somebody on the line said.

"Yeah, they're awful. Ask for the chili. It's homemade," somebody else said.

It didn't matter. Chili, sandwiches, anything sounded good. Carol was too tired to care. Looking toward the sky, the icy misty rain stinging her face, Carol was thankful it hadn't poured. Water dripped from her hat. Her nose was cold and runny. She was miserable. Overhead, high above all the people and the sandbags, between Carol and the leaden sky, a group of grackles was flying, making an awful racket.

You old crows, Carol said to herself, you can fly away and find somewhere else to go but what about all the people here? Feeling bone-tired, she envied the birds.

"Here, catch," somebody said.

Carol turned and wearily took the bag and passed it on.

"There's the chili," someone called.

"Oh, good," Dick answered. "Let's go, girls."

They moved aside and another group took their place.

Near the line a large gray van was parked, and four people were dishing out chili.

Reba talked to an Amish farmer about the dikes. "Will they hold? Do you really think they will?"

"Better hold or everything we've worked for the last four days will be flooded under about four feet of water."

"Did you see the pictures on national TV? They showed water rushing right through a person's living room window," somebody said.

"That could have been my house in Auburn," Reba said.

"No, it was in Fort Wayne," the person answered. They were standing close to each other, talking, shivering, trying to stay warm, dripping, tired, yet excited.

"I heard the mayor might come survey the situation," a boy said.

"I heard it might be the governor," somebody else said.

"Just imagine," Reba said, "the governor of Indiana!"

"I've never seen anybody famous," Carol said. "Not even the mayor of Fort Wayne."

"Except on television," Dick said.

"Well, of course on television! I've even seen the president of the United States on television, silly," Carol retorted.

Mr. Van Houston came over to the kids. "You've worked hard and we appreciate it. If you can stay, we can use the help. Anyway, thanks for helping."

"Who did you say he is?" Reba asked.

"I don't know. Some volunteer with the Civil Defense, I think. He's wearing a yellow helmet with that Civil Defense sign on it."

"Well, I'm glad we came. I hate to leave, even if I am tired," Dick said. "I could probably work a little longer."

Carol looked up. Her minister was still in line tossing sacks. He looked exhausted.

Dick followed her look. "I'll talk with Pastor Samuels. Might as well get back in line for a while."

"Okay," said Reba.

They went back to the line, but it was going so well, they hated to butt in. "Let's move on down here a little," Carol said. She and Reba wandered down the hill behind the line of sandbaggers. They found a place near some trees and a little rise in the ground. Beyond them was the river. Across the river they could see houses submerged up to their windowsills.

"Where are you from?" someone asked.

"Auburn," the girls answered.

"Catch."

"Got it. Here, Reba."

"Where are you from?" Carol asked the girl.

"Waterloo."

"Oh, that's close to us."

"How long have you been here?" the girl asked.

"Just today. We came today."

"I've been working for three days. This is my third day. I'm really bushed. This is a mess."

"Here, catch."

"Got it, Reba. Here's another one. Pass it on."

"I work in that store back there. We've been trying to get this place sandbagged so if the river crests tonight, it won't come in. If the dikes go, of course, we're ruined. I mean, they are."

The girl pointed to a man and woman who were working side by side. "They're the owners."

They were silent, passing the bags to one another. A heavy dampness made them cold and uncomfortable. Still they worked. Carol glanced at Reba. Their movements were automatic. Catch a sack, pass it on, catch another one.

Carol was aware of people moving around her, coming, going. She wasn't sure of the time. She knew Dick could find them, but it did seem like a long time since he'd left.

Carol started to ask Reba about the time, but remembered Reba didn't have a watch. Glancing again at Reba, she noticed the grim look on Reba's face.

Maybe she's thinking about her own home, Carol thought. Reba's home was a disaster. What would Reba's parents do? She'd have to talk with Reba about that later.

Hunger gnawed at Carol, and she remembered how long it had been since breakfast. That little bit of chili wasn't enough. Her mother's supper would sure taste good, no matter what it was.

Carol began slipping. She shifted her foot to get a better stand and discovered she was up to her ankles in mud. She was glad she'd worn high rubber boots. It was getting colder, rain sputtering from time to time. Everything was wet. People moved behind her. Another group came forward. Carol handed Reba a sack and turned to get another from the girl from Waterloo. The girl was looking at a man beyond her. Carol turned to get a better look. The man was wearing a raincoat. There were several men around him wearing dress suits.

That's odd, Carol thought. *No one would come out here all dressed up, would they? Maybe some businessmen from town had stopped by to survey the situation.* She saw a reporter from a television station. Then she saw a cameraman.

"Bet he's the mayor," Carol said to Reba, who was also watching.

"Or the governor," Reba said.

"It's Reagan!" somebody said.

"Who?"

"President Reagan!"

"President Reagan?" Carol asked looking at Reba then back at the man. "You mean the president of the United States?"

"Mr. President," somebody said, "be careful where you stand. It's pretty muddy here."

Carol stared. The president was wearing a pair of rubber boots and was up to his ankles in mud. He was carefully trying not to slip. He looked around, took another step, and stood directly in front of Carol.

Looking at the river, the sandbaggers, and the crowd, he waved briefly.

Someone passed him a sandbag. "Catch, Mr. president."

"Got it. Here, I'll pass it on."

The president of the United States turned and passed the sandbag to Carol.

Chapter 11

CAROL gasped but took the sandbag from the president and passed it on to Reba. President Reagan gave her a friendly smile, and Carol saw strength and compassion in his eyes. When someone warned the president about the dike, soggy and barely holding, suddenly Carol sensed the danger. It was scary. What if Pemberton Dike broke? What if something happened to the president? Carol felt jittery. Would the dike hold? She was more concerned about him than herself.

Reaching out to catch the sandbag, she said, "Be careful, Mr. President."

"Thanks, I'm trying to be," he answered and handed her another sandbag.

"Do you think," Carol said cautiously, "that we'll be able to get help?"

"This situation is serious. I'm going to consider this immediately," the president said firmly.

Someone held an umbrella over the president's head even though it had stopped sprinkling.

"My friend over there," Carol continued anxiously, pointing to Reba, "lost everything. Her house has water in it up to the kitchen counter. Her dad's out of work. They don't have any money. It's awful."

"Yes, it is," the president said. "I can see it's bad, a real disaster." He handed her another sandbag.

Carol was vaguely aware that a camera was going. Somehow it was more important to tell the president about Reba than pay attention to that stupid camera. She continued, "In Fort Wayne, over 800 families have been evacuated. There has been thousands and thousands of dollars of damage. I don't know what we're going to do. You've got to help us. Please help us."

The president looked at Carol squarely. "My young friend, I want you to know, and all of you out there to know, that if it weren't for thousands of people like you who have volunteered and helped during this disaster, Fort Wayne and northeast Indiana would be in worse shape. You have done your city and country a great service. I am proud of you."

Again President Reagan smiled at Carol. He shook her hand and said, "Congratulations. Keep up the good work. You're a fine citizen, a good American. Good luck. I'll do what I can."

He moved on down the line. Carol stood still for a moment. Then turning to Reba, she said quietly, "Oh, Reba." Reba hugged her. "I don't believe it! I don't believe it! President Reagan! The president of the United States! Here in Fort Wayne!"

People were cheering, some jumping up and down. The president spoke to a few other workers including the girl from Waterloo. Then in a matter of minutes he was gone.

"We heard he was coming," someone shouted.

"Yeah, we heard it was going to be somebody important, but who would have thought it would be President Reagan!" Dick said. "I thought it might be the governor!"

They watched the men move down the line, turn back toward the president's limousine, and wave.

Suddenly Carol realized how excited she was. "The president! I don't believe it! He was right here next to me! He shook my hand! He talked to me! Reba, can you believe what happened? I told him about your dad and your house. He'll help us!"

They grouped together talking excitedly. "This has been the most exciting day of my life," Reba exclaimed.

"And I'd never even seen the mayor of Fort Wayne. Can you imagine?" Carol could hardly believe what happened. She waved good-bye to the girl from Waterloo. Several people waved back and shouted, "Thanks, thanks for helping."

Carol, Reba, and Dick moved back up the line where the others from their church were waiting. They all crowded around telling Carol what they had seen! Everyone was thrilled.

"Imagine us, a little group from the middle of middle America, and we met the president of the United States!" their minister said.

Carol felt trembly with excitement, but she was so tired, all she wanted was to sit down, get home, get warm, eat supper, and go to bed. "Let's go," she said heading for the van.

Mrs. Norton met the group at the church.

"Carol, I saw you on the news! Honey, I can't believe it! You were talking to the president of the United States!"

"Mom, I'm hungry. What's for supper?"

"How can you think of food at a time like this? Nina can't

111

wait to see you. She wants your autograph. She's got a million questions to ask; we all do."

"Oh, that Nina!" Carol laughed. "I'll give her my autograph, sure." Carol turned, "Reba, we should have asked the president for his autograph!"

"Yeah, but we forgot. Besides, we didn't have pencils or anything. I never thought about it. Phooey!"

"Oh, well," Carol said, "at least we saw him."

"What do you mean 'saw' him? You talked to him!"

"I'm so proud of you," Carol's mother said. She positively glowed.

"Let's get home, mom."

"Okay. Dad's home with Nina. Supper is waiting, and some woman called."

"Who?"

"Some woman from the paper. She'd like to interview you."

"Oh, mom, that's crazy."

They drove home and half way there, the rain began to fall, a hard pounding on the roof of the car.

"Just in the nick of time," Reba said leaning back in the car. "Can you believe it?"

"For us, but not for the others. They're still down there, mom. That girl from Waterloo has been working for three days," Carol said.

"The rivers are supposed to crest late tonight. They expect two more inches of rain. I don't know," Millie said, turning into the driveway, "it's been only one week since all this started, but it seems like months."

"This time last week," Reba agreed, "we could hardly get around because of the piles of snow."

"It was a record winter as far as the snow was concerned," Millie agreed. "Here we are."

112

There was a clamor when Reba and Carol walked in the house.

"You were on television," Nina shouted.

"With the president of the United States!" Walt added. "I couldn't believe my eyes!"

"We were so proud," Millie said. "There you were with all those kids and the camera showed how hard everyone was working. Then they panned the camera and showed the president."

"Did he come just for this?" Carol asked.

"No, yes, I guess so. He was on his way home from Oklahoma, and he detoured by Fort Wayne to check the damage. He said he'd seen the flood on the news and wanted to see for himself. You know we've requested Federal assistance. I think he wanted to see firsthand," Walt explained.

"I watched when his plane landed and everything," Nina said. "I knew he was going to see the dikes and the sandbaggers. I bet I knew before you did."

"You did," Reba answered. "We heard somebody important was going to come by, but who would have imagined it would be President Reagan? I was so excited, I couldn't say a word. I would have died if he had spoken to me." Reba looked at Carol with admiration. "But you—you actually talked to him! Like a regular person!"

Carol stretched. "Yeah, it was great. I'm really tired and sore. I don't feel like it really happened. Do you know what I mean?"

"It'll probably take you a couple of days to realize everything," Millie said, putting her arm around Carol. "Come on, supper is ready. I can see you girls are beat."

"You know something, dad," Carol said looking around. "It was exciting. I mean really exciting. Wonderful and all, but I didn't have anything to do with it. It was a coincidence. It was just luck, I guess."

"You were at the right place at the right time," Nina said.

"You'll remember this as long as you live," her dad said proudly. "It was a rare experience. I'm happy for you. I had mixed feelings about your being down there in all that confusion, but I'm glad you went."

"You should have seen the people," Reba said. "People didn't know how to start, but once they got in line, there was plenty to do."

"Somebody brought coffee and sandwiches," Carol said, "but we didn't stop. Then when the homemade chili came, we had some."

"It was good, too. Especially since we were so cold."

"Who else went?" Millie asked.

"About ten people with our group. I don't know. Janice wasn't there. At least I didn't see her."

"Mary Tree wasn't there," Nina said. "I saw her today."

"She told me she was going," Carol said. "I wonder why she didn't. I'll call her later." It seemed like years since she'd talked to Mary. Carol remembered Mary's invitation to Disney World. She decided not to mention it in front of Reba. All she wanted was to eat, stretch out, and rest. Meat loaf and potatoes and salad, what a feast! It was good to be home.

"Let's go to bed, Reba," Carol said later.

"Okay."

The girls were asleep by the time Nina went up to get her sleeping bag.

"Mom," Nina said, "they're out. It's good to have Reba here. I hope she can stay longer."

Early Friday morning, Reba shook Carol. "Wake up. Get up. It's still raining."

114

"Oh, no," Carol said rubbing her eyes. "Wonder how the dikes are?"

They turned on the radio. ". . . and volunteers worked through the night and in spite of the rain, the dikes are still holding! The teenagers of Fort Wayne have saved the city!" the announcer said. "Heroic effort on the part of school-children, teenagers, unemployed adults, and help from willing volunteers from neighboring communities has saved Pemberton Dike. They worked all night and rebuilt it when it started to go. Some 25,000 sandbags were placed every hour and over 6,000 homes saved. It was truly Fort Wayne's finest hour of community cooperation, and we're proud!"

The announcer described the sandbagging operations as Carol and Reba got ready for school. They tiptoed over Nina who was still asleep on the living room floor and muttered how lucky she was to have school in the afternoon.

In the kitchen, Millie had breakfast waiting. The television was on, and the mayor of Fort Wayne was being interviewed.

"We're hoping to get Federal Assistance," he said, "but right now we're continuing to work and watch the rivers. They should crest any time now, and even though the dikes are holding, we're not finished. It is still very dangerous."

"Can it get worse?" Carol asked.

"Can we go back down there?" Reba wanted to know.

"No, girls. I want you in school. And, according to the clock, you'd better hurry."

The girls ate their breakfast and were soon on their way. Water gushed out of rain sewers, stood in swirling pools, and splashed as cars drove carefully through standing water. Evidence of flooding was everywhere. It was spooky, and when the bus crossed Ninth Street Bridge, the students held their breath. It seemed water was lapping their feet. Rain was making it hard to see and large droplets ran down the windows.

"I hope it stops raining soon," Reba said. "I wonder what my dad is doing."

"Probably at the house," Carol said.

"I don't know," Reba answered, "but they know where I am. I'm sure they'll call if they need me." She bit her lip.

"Where's Dick today?" Carol asked.

"I think he went back to help do more sandbagging," Reba said. "He was talking about going again."

"And Mary Tree? I wonder if she went."

"I doubt it," Reba said. "She'll do anything she wants, though."

"What do you mean? She's not all bad," Carol said defensively.

"I know that. I just mean she'll go if she wants. Her mom doesn't care much what she does."

"Really? And how do you know?"

"She talks. She told me she'd give a million if her mom cared enough about her to do anything other than 'buy' her things."

"Come on. She didn't say that, did she?"

"It's true, Carol. Mary told me the other day her mom is letting her go to Florida this spring with her uncle and aunt because she simply couldn't abide having her around for a whole week."

"I don't believe it!"

"Then ask her," Reba said. "She'll tell you."

Carol wondered whether she should mention Mary Tree's invitation to Reba. She decided not to. She had mixed feelings about the whole situation.

When they got off the school bus, the bell was ringing. It had taken them longer because traffic was so slow.

"See ya," Carol called.

"Okay," Reba answered.

"Well, hello, Miss Celebrity," Janice teased. "You're lucky. I can't believe it. Right next to the president and you talked to him, too!"

"Janice, it was fun. Really, but it was just one of those things."

"Listen to that. Just one of those things! You must be joking. Talking to the president of the United States isn't just one of those things!"

"Would you give us an interview?" Eldon asked, coming up behind Carol. He was wearing a nice pair of jeans and a checked shirt. He looked so handsome, Carol nearly gulped. He'd spoken to her! She felt more trembly and excited than when she'd talked with the president.

"Well, yes, I guess so."

"When can we meet?" Eldon looked at his watch. "You'll make a great feature story for the paper."

He was in the eleventh grade and feature editor of the paper. He was vice-president of the Pep Club, and the boy voted most handsome in his class. He was talking to Carol!

"How . . . how about during my study hall?" she volunteered. "I could do it then."

"Super! Fine! I'll meet you then. They'll excuse you for an interview. No problem." Eldon flashed a wide smile at her. Carol could hardly say, "See ya."

As he turned away, Carol saw how the other girls looked at her.

"Oh, wow!" Janice said. "Chalk one up for you!"

"Yeah," Carol said quickly. "I'll take that point any day."

But, inside, Carol was as nervous as a turkey before Thanksgiving.

Chapter 12

CAROL could hardly keep her mind on her work. People talked to her who had never spoken to her before. Teachers made comments about how calm she'd been when talking to President Reagan. Even the principal made an announcement saying how proud he was of his students and especially proud that Carol Norton had represented DeKalb High School so well.

Carol was happy but somehow felt the event didn't deserve so much attention. Nevertheless, she whispered to Reba during lunch, "How do you think I'm doing?"

Reba whispered back, "Great, I'm proud of you."

Mary Tree had slipped close and overheard Carol's question. She also answered, "Super, Carol. Play it up. You're important. Be the star!"

Carol smiled a little and shook her head. The way Mary Tree spoke bothered her. Sure all the comments made her feel important, but she didn't deserve them. It had been a coincidence in the first place. She sharpened her pencil, her mind whirling. How should I act? Be nonchalant? Be important? In the back of her mind she kept remembering her mother's words, "Be yourself."

Those words made sense in most situations, but with Eldon Newiston, "herself" seemed a bit plain. He didn't talk to just anyone, and everybody knew he'd been around. She'd better act more sophisticated.

She checked the clock. In ten minutes she'd be in study hall. *I'll play the role to the hilt,* she decided. She checked her hair. It was windblown. She tried to smooth it down. She'd barely have time to duck into the restroom and comb it quickly.

Carol hurried. She was glad she'd had her hair trimmed two weeks earlier, and she was pleased the way the light made it shine. She pinched her cheeks to make them rosier, and smiled. For someone fifteen years old, blue-eyed, with brown shoulder-length hair, she looked pretty sharp. In fact, and it almost shocked her, there seemed a polished assurance about her. Good. Inside I may be quaking, but at least I look confident. What had happened? Just two weeks before she remembered complaining bitterly about how awful she looked.

It's the excitement, the compliments, Eldon, she thought. *Funny how a popular person seems more popular just because she is or people think she is. I must remember to explain this to Reba,* she thought. *All a person has to do is get some of the limelight and the other comes. It's almost like magic. And to think, all these years I've wondered how to look popular. Now I know,* she thought excitedly, *now I know!* She made a mental note to tell Reba about it later. As the bell rang, she hurried to her table.

"Where were you?" Janice asked Carol. "I didn't have

time to talk to you last period. Would you like to come over this afternoon and play records?"

"I'm not sure, Janice. It depends." Carol wondered briefly why Janice was asking in the first place. Janice was ambitious and smart. Not only was she popular but also had the best grades of anyone in the class. Carol thought about the many times she'd wished Janice would ask her to do something, but Janice always seemed busy. Janice ran around with the smartest kids in class, the most talented ones, and the best liked. "I'll let you know," Carol said.

Maybe I should go to her house and get to know her, Carol thought. On the other hand, she knew Janice as well as she wanted to know her. Reba had said it so well, "Janice will like you and hang around with you if she thinks it will make her look good."

Carol had to agree. Janice could sure play it both ways. Carol and Reba had already decided Janice would waltz right out of school with the top awards, the really big ones.

As Carol thought about Janice, Eldon came to the door and spoke to Mrs. Spivy. Mrs. Spivy looked at the note and nodded at Carol.

"You have an appointment, I believe, Carol. You may use my office across the hall."

While everyone watched, Carol walked to the door. With Eldon watching, everyone looking, Carol hoped she could make it without tripping or stumbling. She took a deep breath and felt herself moving toward the door almost as in a dream.

In the hall outside the view of some thirty people, Carol realized she was still nervous. Here she was with Eldon, a guy she'd often thought about. She hoped she wouldn't make a fool of herself.

"Let's go in Mrs. Spivy's room," Eldon said. He was smiling and friendly. "I've got a few questions to ask you," he said.

"Okay." Carol sat in the chair close to the door.

"Are you comfortable? Do you want to put your books on the desk?"

Eldon sat at the table and opened a small note pad. "How do you feel about being interviewed?"

"I've never been before, at least not yet," Carol said.

"Waited until something pretty outstanding happened to you to make it worthwhile, right?" Eldon laughed. "And it was outstanding, don't you think?"

"I guess," Carol said.

"What do you think you would say if you had the chance to relive that experience, to speak to the president again?"

"I don't know. Probably the same thing I said before."

"And exactly what did you say?" Eldon was looking at her curiously.

Carol knew he wanted a statement, something dynamic he could print. It irritated her that he seemed so anxious, so eager. He was waiting for her answer.

"I'd probably say Mr. President, you see the need here. Flooding has caused hundreds of families to be evacuated. The damage to our streets and homes is terrible. If possible, could you consider Federal Assistance?"

Eldon shifted in his chair. "On television I heard you say something a little more dramatic. There was an intensity in the way you spoke. I'd like to recapture that here."

"Well, I was surprised," Carol answered, "to see the president, and at first I didn't think of him as the president. Somehow I felt he had to *know*, to *understand* our situation."

"Let me think out loud," Eldon said with a faint smile, leaning back to look at Carol. "If you were interviewing somebody who had given a very convincing speech over national television about our flood, what would you ask?"

Carol knew Eldon was trying to manipulate her comments. Nervously she picked at the edge of the desk blotter. The interview wasn't anything like she expected. On the other hand, she had to admit, she'd never given a thought about what questions would be asked or how she should answer them. She'd been too busy worrying about her hair and how she looked.

I'd better get this together, she thought hastily, *or Eldon will think I'm a flea-brain.* She remembered something a newscaster had said, so taking a deep breath, she spoke, trying to keep her voice steady. Her heart was thumping so loud she knew Eldon could hear it.

"I believe that if I were given a chance to speak with the president again, I would explain not only the need we have for Federal Aid, but emphasize the importance of Washington being responsive to middle America, the problems at the grass roots, the taxpayers and the work they have done to establish support in the corridors of Washington."

Carol took another deep breath. She was sure her answer was what Eldon wanted. Or was it? He was looking at her with a strange question in his eye. Was it respect? She'd used some pretty fancy phrases. She hoped she'd gotten them right.

"What about your particular day in Fort Wayne," Eldon asked. "What made you decide to go? Were you involved somehow with a special family or was it an intrinsic need to participate on a larger scale?"

"I went to Fort Wayne because there was an appeal for help. A group from our church went, and yes, I wanted to get involved."

Carol wasn't pleased with her answer. It wasn't anything

122

she said but a feeling about how she was talking and using words. Somehow Eldon definitely wasn't getting the kind of interview she was sure he wanted. She waited for his next question. Would it be about how the president looked? The dog tired work involved? She waited.

Eldon put his note pad away. A slight frown crossed his face. Then he smiled. "Would you like to have a Coke?"

"Oh, yes," Carol said. Her mouth was so dry and parched, a soft drink, water, anything would be great. "Thank you," she croaked.

"I'll get us one." He fished around for some coins and said, "I'll be back."

Carol wondered if she should offer to pay for her pop. She didn't know so she took out her purse and waited. *This whole thing isn't going right,* she thought. *It's too stilted, it's me, it's the way I'm acting.*

"Here you are," Eldon said handing her the Coke. "I was getting thirsty myself."

"Thanks, here's the money."

"Oh, no, my treat," Eldon said. "Besides, I'm interviewing you, remember?"

They sipped the Cokes. Carol felt a terrible silence descend upon them, but Eldon seemed perfectly relaxed. He was probably used to interviewing weird people, nervous people. This was probably a technique. Start the interview, relax the person, get them to talk. Carol couldn't seem to get her thoughts together, and it irritated her. *If we could just get this over with,* she thought moodily.

"Let me tell you something," Eldon said. "Interviewing people is tough, but I like it. I like you too. You're really trying, I can see that, but listen, don't worry so much about what you're saying or how you're saying it. I just want to talk about your experiences. Like, did you feel the president understood what you were trying to say to him? Did he sense the urgency of the situation?"

"Yes, I think he did," Carol said lamely. She was absolutely blowing the interview. She was using stilted dumb phrases like "the corridors of Washington," on the one hand. On the other, she seemed too flea-brained when she tried to relax. All she could say then was yes, no, great. It made her mad. Remembering her mother's advice about being herself she began to talk.

"Look, when the president came by, I was totally surprised. I really hadn't expected anybody, not the mayor, nobody. Really I just went to Fort Wayne with a bunch of other kids from my church. It was exciting, a real adventure. But it was a coincidence. I had nothing to do with it."

There, it was out. Carol knew the interview was no good. She'd done nothing important. It had been just luck. Oh, well, no use trying to impress Eldon now. Shrugging her shoulders, she continued, " . . . so we worked with the sandbagging, and the more we worked, the more involved we got. It was like a fight. It was probably silly to think that one person could make a difference in saving the entire city of Fort Wayne from flooding, but I got caught up in it. You know, the more I worked and saw the mess, the more I knew I couldn't stop until I'd done everything I could. Anyway there I was, and I looked up and there stood the president. He was in line, and he handed me a sandbag like he'd been doing it all day . . . except he had on a suit. He was wearing some boots somebody lent him and he was working and I was working. That's the way it was."

She started to get up. She'd blown her chance to sound important, "to play it like a star," as Mary Tree had said. So what? Now if she could get back to study hall, she'd have time to get her math done.

"Wait a minute," Eldon said. "Tell me, when you saw President Reagan next to you, did you get nervous or anything?"

"I was too tired to think about it. He seemed so natural and there was a kind look in his eyes, a look I'll never forget. I thought maybe he was scared with all that water and the possible danger. It could have been bad, you know. But it wasn't fear I noticed. I think it was a kind of hurt, a hurting for all he saw, for the people working so hard in such a terrible situation, and at the same time, he was proud. Maybe I imagined part of it, but there were a lot of feelings about how good it was to be an American, to work together for something. I don't know, but I've seen that same look in my dad's face, like on Memorial Day or the Fourth of July, parades, you know?"

Eldon sat quietly looking at Carol.

"Well, I guess that's it. I'll go now."

"No, don't. I'd like to talk to you some more. Have you ever done much writing or anything connected with our newspaper?"

"No."

"You might want to think about it. You have insight, and I think you could handle some features."

"I—I never thought about it." Carol was surprised. "Besides, how do you know I can put anything down on paper?"

"We'll get to that. I know you're in Mr. Fowler's class and that says a lot. He's good about advising students. I had Mr. Fowler myself. He's tough but he's good," Eldon said. "You don't have to decide now. Just think about it. Next year I'll be in charge of the paper."

"I don't know. I've never thought about it, but it does sound exciting. Are you sure?"

"Sure I'm sure. You've got a way with people, and that's good. It's an asset."

"How about my interview? It was pretty dumb, wasn't it? Not what you wanted."

"I'll have to admit at first you were nervous. But then so was I. After all, it isn't every day I get a chance to interview somebody who talked with the president."

"You were nervous?"

"You bet. It'll make a great feature. Just wait."

Carol grinned. Then she remembered Eldon probably said all that just to get a good story. Some line! What a dope she'd been!

"Hope I answered your questions okay. I've got to go," she said curtly. She stood up and left. Eldon was still sitting at the table.

"Fat jerk!" she muttered to herself. Back in study hall, she tried to think about her work, but her mind kept going over and over the interview. Nothing had gone wrong. But neither had anything gone right. What did he think of her? Had he used her experience just to get a great story? What a dope she'd been to blurt out her thoughts and feelings. Carol felt humiliated and embarrassed.

"How did it go?" Reba asked on their way home.

"Okay."

"I mean how was Eldon? Nice?"

"I don't know. I don't care."

"You crazy or something?"

"I might have been a failure. Maybe I did okay. Who cares?"

"I can't believe this," Reba said. "All year long you've talked about Eldon Lewiston. You said you'd die if he would as much as look at you. Now you spend some twenty minutes with him, and you don't care?"

"So."

"So tell me about it," Reba insisted.

"At first I was so nervous I couldn't say a thing. Then when I did talk I sounded awful. I used some fancy dumb words."

"Then?"

"Then I got so frustrated, I blurted out some things. Pretty dumb, huh?"

"I don't know. What did he say?"

"He said I had insight." Carol looked at Reba, "Insight. Can you believe that?"

"Insight! But that's great. That was a compliment. See, he saw you for what you are, a sensitive person. I've known that all the time."

"You think so?"

"Yeah. That makes me think maybe Eldon isn't so fancy himself."

"What do you mean, fancy?"

"You know, people say he's so with it, so self-assured. Maybe he's not conceited after all."

"Who said Eldon was conceited?" Carol demanded.

"I don't know. I thought you said he was conceited."

"I never said he was that way. I just said he didn't know I existed."

"Well he knows you do now!" Reba looked at Carol and grinned. "I'll bet he'll speak to you tomorrow."

Carol shrugged and smiled. "Well, maybe. He seemed nice. Guess what? He bought me a Coke."

"He did? Fabulous! See, he liked you!"

"Well, he got himself one. He said he was thirsty. No big deal."

"Fiddle!"

"Reba, promise you won't tell? He asked me to think

about working on the paper next year when he s editor."

"You're joking? Really?"

"No," Carol said proudly. "I told him I'd think about it."

"Think about it? You serious? I don't believe this. You played that just right!"

"I didn't play anything. I just told him what I thought."

"I think you like him a lot," Reba said, poking at Carol.

"I don't know. Maybe, I guess so. Say Reba, who do you like a lot, as if I couldn't guess?"

"You really want to know, huh? Dick."

"I knew it," Carol laughed. "I just knew it!"

The bus stopped, and the girls got out trying not to step in the standing water.

"At least this water isn't getting higher," Reba said. "And look at that clear blue sky! Spring's here, don't you think?"

"Yeah, and so is Dick. Here he comes. Shall I walk ahead so the two of you can talk?"

"No," said Reba. "He doesn't want to talk to me. He likes you."

"You're just saying that. That's not true. It couldn't be."

"No, I'm not," Reba said. "I can tell he likes you. I'm not stupid, you know."

"Well, personally I disagree with you."

"We'll see," Reba said zipping up her jacket.

"Hi, girls," Dick called.

"Hi to you," Carol answered. "Have you had enough of this water?"

"Enough and more than enough!"

They laughed and pretended to splash each other.

"Hey, Carol," Dick continued, "can I talk to you for a minute? Privately? There's something I want to ask."

Chapter 13

"TELL me, Carol, why won't Reba talk to me? You're a good friend. Do I have bad breath or something? Everytime I try to talk to her, she hurries away."

Carol was surprised. "She's shy, Dick. I never knew her until this last week. She's had a hard time. Her family has. You like her, don't you?"

"How can I say I like her or not? I can hardly talk to her. I asked her about her house and she said, 'I can't give you a civil answer about our house!' Then she walked away."

"Oh, Dick, she's upset. Her house is totally ruined. They won't be able to live there anymore. All she owns can go in one suitcase and two cardboard boxes."

"Maybe that explains it, but why won't she give me the time of day?"

"She's been with us almost a week now, but she can't believe anyone, except maybe us, really cares about her. Give her another try. She's hurt."

"She's hurt? From the flood? She's not alone! That hurt us all!"

"Not the same way. Her dad's been out of work for almost a year. Things are really bad. She bottles it all up, worries about it. Mom said unemployment is like a family crisis, like death or a serious illness."

"Well...."

"Talk to her again."

"That's a laugh. I'll try, but she really clams up. We ride the bus together, we're in the same classes, my brother's been laid off from International Harvester for months, and besides, we both got flooded pretty bad."

"Not as bad as she did."

"You're right. We got water in the basement, but nothing like her place."

Carol looked into Dick's blue eyes and noticed the warm freckles across his nose. His light hair somehow reminded her of summer. It hit her with a jolt that she'd never thought of him as special, but he was really sweet.

"Yeah, Dick, Reba's nice, a real friend. See you later."

"Bye. And say, Carol? You're great. Thanks."

Carol hurried to catch Reba.

"Well, what did he want? An interview?" Reba joked.

"You kidding, Reba? You'd fall over with shock if you only knew! He'd like to get to know you better, but he said you won't ever talk to him. You know something? You're a bit whacky to always put him off. Can't you be friendly or something?" Carol was annoyed. "Reba, do you know what's wrong with you? You're stuck up."

"What do you mean, stuck up? Carol, I can't believe you're saying this. That's an awful thing to say, and I don't like it one bit! All of a sudden, too. What did that Dick Moore say?" Reba was angry.

"Nothing, except you won't talk to him. You know something, Reba? It makes me mad. You could have friends all over the place. You say you aren't popular. The problem is you. You aren't fair. You don't give people a chance. You never gave me a chance. You just wrote me off."

"I can't imagine, I—I. . . . What have I done?"

"You've been too smug, that's what."

"Smug? I don't believe this!"

"Yeah, feeling sorry for yourself. Dick says everytime he tries to talk to you, you clam up. Now why would people want to be friendly? Like Dick said, you put them off."

"Dick said that?" Reba clutched her books. "I didn't know that's the way I seemed. I guess I was afraid. I guess I thought they'd think I was different," she said lamely. "You're right, Carol. I didn't give them much of a chance."

Carol thought for a minute. "You know the word 'popular'? Well, there's no such thing as being popular, just like that. It's not attention that you get or have to have. Not really. People react to kindness, Reba. You're popular when people like you, and people like people who are kind and loyal and friendly. It's not something magic, you know. If you like people, they'll like you. It's a two-way street." Carol kicked a pebble and watched it splash into some water. "My mom's got a saying, 'The world is a looking glass that gives back the reflection of anyone's face.' "

"Your mom's a peach, Carol. She's got a saying for everything!"

"Reba, you're like a sister to me. Here I am fussing at you, but I'm really going to miss you when you go back to your place. I can talk to you. I really like you. Get to know Dick. He's genuine. He likes you too."

Reba was silent for a moment. "Genuine? Did I hear you say that? The other day you called him a stuffed shirt."

"He's genuine. I don't care what I called him. I've known him since we were in nursery school."

"Eldon's nice too," Reba volunteered.

"Yeah, but he's not for me. We both know that."

"You can have Dick...."

"No, Reba. That's not it. I'm going to keep my eyes open and not be so anxious to write people off. Like you, I never give some of them a chance."

"Mary Tree?" Reba asked.

"Nah. I don't know. She's a gossip. I'm not talking about her or Janice or anyone in particular. I'm just saying from now on I'm going to take my time before deciding how I feel about people."

"Everybody has good and bad points, I guess. I'm sorry I was so—so standoffish. I didn't mean to act that way."

"It's okay. I'm really not upset, Reba. I just have this problem. I'm too quick to judge."

"I could change too. I'd like to be easier with people. I'd really like to talk to Dick. I thought you'd not like me if I talked to your boyfriend."

"What do I care? Dick's just a friend. Guess we're crazy, talking like this. I wonder what mom's having for supper?"

"Spaghetti, I hope. She makes great spaghetti and meatballs. Carol, my mom makes the best beef and noodles. You'll have to come over and have some."

"Supper or dinner?"

"Well, silly, if you come and act like company, we'll have to call it dinner. Otherwise...."

"But if I come over, Reba, I just want to be a friend."

"Then it doesn't matter. We'll call it...."

"Supper!" The girls laughed.

"Mom usually has something cooking by this time," Carol said sniffing. "I don't smell a thing."

"Maybe it's in the freezer," Reba volunteered.

"Yeah, probably. *Nina?*" Carol called. "Where's mom?"

"At the hospital! She left a note," Nina said, running down the stairs. "Here read it. It says heat the frozen chicken casserole. Nothing serious. Not to worry."

"Why did she go? I wonder," Carol fumed.

"I'm hungry," Nina said. She began looking through the refrigerator. "Want some sandwich spread?"

"Yeah, let's make sandwiches. Get the bread, Reba."

"There's no bread in here," Reba said closing the breadbox. "I'll check the freezer."

"None in there," Nina said.

"That's not like mom," Carol said.

"Well, use crackers, then. I do that all the time at home," Reba said.

The girls ate their snack by the patio door where they could see the flood plain.

"The water's gone down some," Nina said, "but not much. It still looks like a lake out there."

"It's going to seem funny all dried up," Carol said. "I've gotten used to this."

"Can you believe it covered the grape arbor?" Nina pointed for Reba to see. "I'm going to miss the old mallards."

The phone rang. "It's for you, Reba," Carol said.

Reba took the receiver. "Hi, dad," she said. "Yeah, I'm okay. Yeah, I miss being with you and mom too. Still at Aunt Gretchen's?" See paused. "You're *what?* Really? That's great! I'll help."

Nina and Carol were curious.

"Dad said he's going to try a feed and seed store again some day. He talked to a man who's willing to help him."

"Great!" the girls exclaimed.

"More than that," Reba said. "Dad sounded like his old self. He didn't yell. He wanted to tell me himself. He said mom was lying down. Thought maybe I should come home and help."

"Do you think things will work out?" Carol asked.

"I don't know. We'll live in the country for a while. We'll be able to get some help . . . the Red Cross and all."

"Wish you could stay with us," Nina said.

"So do I, in a way," Reba said thoughtfully. "But I really have missed my family."

"Stay until the weekend, Reba, next weekend," Carol said. "You're like family. I'll miss you."

"You are family to me," Reba answered. "You really are."

The girls looked at each other. "The old flood made us friends, that's one thing," Carol said.

"The flood! Ha! Do you know I have practically nothing, and I'm feeling grateful! Isn't that funny?" Reba asked.

"Grateful?" Nina wanted to know.

"Yeah, grateful for you two, for your parents, for the talks we've had. So what if I don't have anything but my suitcase and my boxes? At least I won't have to unpack so much."

"It's not the stuff," Nina said, "it's your family."

"Yeah, believe it or not, I actually missed hearing dad yell and mom grumble. Your parents aren't like that, though."

"Yes, but parents are parents," Carol said. "They're all a little crazy."

"Crazy, but we couldn't do without them, could we?" Reba said.

"Too bad mom isn't here to hear *this*," Nina said. "She'd never believe this heavy talk."

A sound hit the door. "That's the paper," Nina said. "I'll get it."

She hurried back and spread it open. The girls crowded to

see the aerial pictures and photographs of the flood. One headline read, "Disaster Center Open Tonight."

"Evacuees should go to the first floor of the courthouse to receive legal and financial help," Carol read.

"My dad's probably down there already," Reba said. "If they declare DeKalb County a disaster area, we'll be able to get federal help—some money."

"I heard dad say the Civil Defense, Red Cross, and the county commissioners, especially one of them, had worked hard to make our particular case known," Carol said.

"You did your part too, Carol," Reba added. "You told the president about me. That must have helped."

"I hope so," Carol said. "I really hope so."

Reba went upstairs with Nina. Carol stared out at the flood plain. Water spread through the trees all the way to the creek. The way Cedar Creek emptied into the St. Joe River had contributed to the flooding in Fort Wayne. It seemed so much had happened in just one week. Mary Tree and her talk about Disney World! It seemed impossible, but Carol hadn't thought of that since the flood.

"Carol," Nina said, coming down again. "Reba's changing into her jeans. Did you know Aunt Madden is thinking about moving to Florida?"

"You're kidding! Aunt Madden? Are you sure? Why?"

"Well, not for good—just during the winter months. She's thinking about it. She said that her friend—that neighbor of hers, Mrs. Val Delague—wants her to be her companion and go south with her during the winters. They've talked about it a lot."

"You mean that French lady, the one with the dog? That Bi—Bichon— Fri— Frise dog? Where in Florida?"

"That dog's a poodle to me," Nina said. "I don't care what she calls it. It's just the cutest little bundle of fluff."

"Yeah, but where in Florida?" Carol asked again.

"Near Orlando."

"Just a couple of months, huh?"

"Yeah, just during the coldest months," she said. "Mrs. Delague's nephew lives down there, but Mrs. Delague doesn't want to move in with him."

"Aunt Madden would probably love going. What about her operation, though?"

"She says she'll be okay by next winter because she's going to take care of that operation right away. I talked to her for a long time today. She's just fifty-five, you know, talks about living a long time yet."

"I believe her. Just think, Nina, we could go to see her. Did you say near Orlando?"

"Yeah."

"That's where Disney World is! Nina, we could see Disney World! Can you believe that? Do you think she'll go?"

"I think so. She's serious about it. Mom says she is."

"That would be unreal! Think about it. We'd be able to travel! You know how mom and dad are. They never go anywhere unless they can visit family."

"Yeah, we could go to Disney World. All of us. The whole family," Nina said happily.

"I hope she goes. Not just because of Disney World, but she'd be happy doing something like that. She doesn't like these winters. And she's been so nervous since Uncle Ben died. I think it would be good for her. I'd really miss her, though."

Nina agreed and shrugged. "Wonder why mom's not home yet?" She went upstairs. Carol thought about her mother at the hospital.

"Oh, dear God," she whispered. "Please don't let it be mom or dad or Aunt Madden." Even though the note said not to worry, Carol knew something had happened. It had to be Aunt Madden. She stood up and leaned her forehead against the patio door. It was cool and she shivered. It just couldn't be Aunt Madden, though. Mom would have told us or dad would have been here. The shadows were long. Night would soon fall. Carol didn't like it when her parents were gone this time of day. The house seemed too empty.

She looked across the flood plain. Opening the door, she wondered if it were getting colder. As she stepped out on the deck, she heard a noise—a strange large flapping sort of noise. From the shadows just beyond the deck, a huge blue bird rose, wings flapping, its long neck arched.

"A blue heron!" Carol exclaimed, recognizing it from pictures. "A great blue heron!" There was a flash of white as the underparts of the wings showed.

The sight took her breath away. It was a magic moment when eternity and the present seemed fused. A flash of beauty on a dreary afternoon! Life was like that. There would always be beauty and magic, even in the middle of trouble and suffering.

Rising from the waters with much flapping, the great blue heron disappeared into the distant trees. Carol remembered her mother's saying, "We sense heaven through life's common things, kinship with God through the windows of nature."

It was true. Carol knew she'd changed. She could be whatever she dreamed. She stood by the door trying to see the heron. She longed to follow its flight, but all she could see was the dark shadow where it landed. She heard her mother calling, but she didn't answer.

"Carol? Carol, come here."

Carol still didn't answer. She didn't move. She knew exactly what she must do.

Chapter 14

"OH, here you are, Carol," Millie said. "It's getting dark."

"I know, mother, I know. But I just saw something. A great blue heron! Right here by our deck! It was huge. It rose with a big flapping noise and flew across the opening into those trees. I wish you could have seen it! It was beautiful!"

Millie was surprised. "That's unusual. I wouldn't think you'd see a heron here. You'll never forget this flood, will you?"

"No, I really won't. I've had some fantastic experiences."

"You've been fortunate."

"Mom, it's getting cold out here."

"Brr, you're right. Let's go inside."

"Where were you?"

"At the hospital. It was Mrs. Gilbert, from church. You know her. She sits so straight and tall, up near the front."

"What happened? Did she die?" Carol remembered Mrs. Gilbert. She did beautiful knitting, and her mom had bought a pair of mittens from her at the church thrift shop. It wouldn't seem right not to see her in church every Sunday.

"No, no. She fell and broke a hip. She lives in an apartment on Eastside. There was water in the yard, and she went out to put a lid on the garbage can and stepped on a rock or a little stone and slipped. I happened to be passing and saw her go down."

"You were there?"

"Like I said, I happened to be driving by and I saw her go down. I called the ambulance. They got her to the hospital. She would have frozen out there. I just thank the Lord I was there. We called her daughter in Columbus, and she'll be here by eight or nine tonight."

"Mother, what a coincidence! I'm glad you were there, too. You sure get involved, don't you?"

"My luck, I guess. When the pot boils, I seem to be around," Millie chuckled. "You know, Carol, it's a wonderful feeling to do a good turn like that."

"I know. I bet she thought it was all over for her when she fell."

"Yes, she said she felt faint, a little dizzy in the wind. Like I said, there was water all over the yard and she was trying to be careful. She slipped and hit the edge of the curb. Got mud all over the clothes. It was a sight! This flood has been disastrous for a lot of people. It's dangerous in more ways than one."

"You've had a busy day. Come on, mom, I'll help get dinner ready."

At the supper table there was a lot of talk.

"Well, I've got some facts to tell too," Walt said. "Over

110 people applied for flood relief here yesterday. The typical flood victim, if there is such a thing, had damages around five thousand dollars. Farmers and businesses had more, of course."

"Too bad we didn't have insurance," Reba said.

"Very few people have flood insurance," Walt said.

"It's going to be a long time before things get back to normal," Millie said. "The county unemployment is 18 percent, the highest in northeast Indiana."

"My dad wants to start a feedstore again," Reba said. "I hope he does. It'll take time though."

"Meanwhile you can pretend to be my sister," Carol said. "Come over here anytime."

"I'm going home this weekend. Mom needs me. She's a nervous wreck. Dad said she's going to try to help, though."

"Really? Your mom agreed to help your dad?" Carol asked.

"Yes, said she had nothing to lose. Said since we have nothing, we may as well start over."

"That's great," Millie said. "Where will you live?"

"For the time being, out with Molly Owens. She's got a big old house in the country. She'll let us live out there if dad will manage the place until it sells. It's temporary."

"That may take months and months. Nothing much is selling these days," Millie remarked.

"Dad used to help Mr. Owens years ago when he raised hogs," Reba continued. "Mrs. Owens is old and lives in the back part of the house. It will be okay."

"Your dad is going to make it, Reba. He's had some hard knocks. I have to admire him. Not many people would keep trying like he does," Walt said, reaching for the salad dressing. "I'm going to talk with him. He'll need all the encouragement he can get."

"It's mom I'm worried about. But if they can work together instead of yelling and fighting about every little thing, that will be great."

"It was fun having you around," Nina said.

"Yeah," Carol said. "We'll help any way we can."

"You've done so much already. We'll never be able to pay you back."

"You would have done it for us," Millie said. "You're welcome anytime. You don't even have to think about paying us back. You're like a daughter to me now."

After dinner, the Nortons listened to the news.

". . . and the Maumee River is continuing to recede, getting down to 23.89 feet, a drop of just over two feet from the high watermark of 25.9 feet. DeKalb County has been declared a federal disaster area due to flooding of Cedar Creek and the St. Joe River. The state is offering grants up to $1,000 for home repair to families who meet low-income standards. Overall, it will take some time before this flood-weary city will get back to normal. Estimates aren't in yet, but damages will be in the millions of dollars."

"That's a lot of money," Reba said. "Wish we had just a little of it."

"Yeah, me too," Nina said. "I'd travel, buy clothes, ice-cream cones, go to Cedar Point. That's *my* favorite place."

"Mom, that reminds me. Is Aunt Madden going to Florida to live? Nina says she is."

"Yes, I think so. She's quite serious about it. We plan to go down and see her next winter."

"I sure will miss her," Carol said, "but at least I'll have her around part of the time."

Carol thought about how it would be without her aunt. "I'm going upstairs," she said. "I've got to call Aunt Madden."

The line was busy. "Rats," Carol said. She looked out the window. The moon was on its side. She could see light glimmering on the water in the flood plain. *If only I were an artist*, she thought.

She dialed Mary Tree.

"Mary, I've decided I'm not going to Florida with you this spring."

"Not going? You must be crazy," Mary Tree said.

"No, I'm going with my family next year."

"You're a drag," Mary complained. "Now I'll have to hang around Aunt Tildy and Uncle Jason all the time. Ah, come on, Carol, it won't cost you anything."

"Ask somebody else. Ask Reba or Janice."

"I'll ask Janice. She's more like me. Bye." Mary Tree hung up.

"Boy," Carol fumed. "So ask her! I don't care." But in a way, she did. She felt sorry she'd turned down such a fabulous invitation, but deep inside, she felt good about it too.

She dialed her aunt. This time Madden answered.

"Hi, this is Carol. Aunt Madden, can I come talk with you?"

"Right now? Of course, honey, of course. You can talk to me over the phone."

"No. I want to talk to you face to face. I want to tell you something."

"Can't you just tell me now?"

"No, it's got to be in person. See you tomorrow after school. I'll take the bus across town. Good-night, Aunt Madden."

"Good-night, honey."

Carol hurried downstairs. She found her mother folding towels. "Mom, I turned down Mary Tree. I'd rather go to Disney World with the family."

Millie Norton raised her eyebrows. "Are you sure?"

"I'm sure. I'm not like Mary Tree. I like her, but she isn't really my friend."

"Get to know her better, Carol. She's probably nice."

"Yeah, okay, okay. Mom, *when* we go to Florida, *if* we go, can Reba go with us?"

"Yes, I think we can manage that," Millie said putting down the towels. "You want to hug me? Like when you were a kid?"

"Oh, okay. Like when I was a kid." Carol laughed and gave her mother a squeeze. "I'm going to Aunt Madden's after school tomorrow. I've got to talk to her."

"You can talk to me. I'll listen."

"Not this time, mom. It's personal."

"Okay, honey."

Carol went upstairs to her bedroom. While Nina and Reba were talking, Carol looked in her dresser and rummaged around in her jumble of stuff and junk. She found what she was looking for and quickly slipped it into her pocket. *I must give this to Aunt Madden,* she thought, and she hurried to get ready for bed.

Chapter 15

THE next morning at school, Eldon hurried toward Carol. "Check the paper. Your feature's in it."

Carol smiled. "Should I disappear? Is it good?"

"It's fantastic! Even if I did write it myself," Eldon grinned. "Your answers were from the hip, really good."

"Well, you did it. All I did was sandbag. It was a coincidence, you know."

"So what? You were the one it happened to. You talked to the president. You sandbagged. So, you're the one interviewed. Enjoy the notoriety."

"I will," Carol said and she laughed. She felt comfortable with Eldon. He was good-looking and talented, but for some reason, she no longer felt intimidated.

"I've got an idea, Eldon. What do you think about a short column next year about nature?"

"Nature? In our school paper?"

"Yes, why not? It wouldn't have to be long, just a little

window type thing telling about some natural phenomenon."

"Like how the salmon swims upstream and then dies?"

"Yes, or about spiders, birds, whatever."

"I thought we'd feature people, not bugs," Eldon said, eyes twinkling. "Convince me."

"Okay, okay, talk about people, but this could be just a paragraph how nature is a miracle, a wonder. Do you know during the flood, I've seen a groundhog, an opossum, a skunk, mallards, all kinds of animals in our backyard. And guess what? Yesterday about sundown, I saw a great blue heron."

"In your backyard?"

"Yes, all sorts of animals have been back there. It's been interesting." Carol thought for a minute, "Guess I sound like a conservationist or something. Forget it. It's probably silly. I've got to get to class."

"Hey, not so quick. You may have an idea. I'll give it some thought. Glimpses into nature, huh? It would be different. Tell you what. If we do it, you can write the column."

"Really? Oh, wow! Then I'd better get with it in English!"

"Talk to you later, Carol. It has possibilities."

By lunchtime everyone had seen the paper. Carol felt a bit embarrassed by all the attention, but according to Janice, she was doing okay.

Reba made sure she got a copy for her scrapbook and asked Carol for an autograph.

"Sure, sure, for you I'll autograph it. But don't tell anybody I did such a silly thing. Have you seen Dick today, Reba?"

"Yes, we talked this morning. He's getting a group to-

gether to help clean up next week. That's the part that isn't
so glamorous, you know. Want to go? I'm going."

"Yes, sure, I'll help."

After school, Carol caught the bus across town.

"Aunt Madden, I just had to see you," Carol said, hurrying up the steps.

"Well, come on in. What's the matter? I'm glad to see
you. Want some soup? A sandwich?"

"Not right now, thanks. A sandwich would taste good
later." Carol put her books and coat on the sofa. "Aunt
Madden, remember when I was about six or seven and you
gave me a bracelet with a little charm on it? A tiny little
hoe?"

"Sure, that was for your birthday. You still have it?"

"Yes. Tell me that story about your grandmother and the
snake."

"But your mother could tell you. Why didn't you ask
her?"

"You said mom wasn't there when it happened. I want to
hear it from you. It's important. I've got to hear it again."

"Oh, all right. Sure, I'll tell you." Madden made herself
comfortable.

"It was a long time ago when your mother and I were
young. We'd lost our mother due to pneumonia and grandmother took us on. We rarely saw father. He worked on the
railroad, but we missed him. Anyway, there we were on the
farm and one day, early in the morning, Millie walked to a
neighbor's to take some berries or something. I was home
with grandmother, and I went out in the yard to swing while
grandmother was inside getting ready to bake bread. The
swing hung from an old cedar tree that had a sort of opening
or hollow at its base where a part had been cut out."

"The part hit by lightning?"

146

"Yes, well, anyway, it formed a kind of bench, a seat there, and we liked to sit on it. Sometimes Millie would sit in the swing and I would sit on the bench. Sometimes it was the other way around, but we'd go out there and talk. Sometimes we'd sit out there and cry about mama being gone. We felt lonely because it was just the two of us, just us, holding our little bit of family together. By the way, grandmother told us she'd lost a penny near that tree as a small girl so lots of times Millie and I talked about finding that coin. We'd even dig around the tree, but we never found it.

"Anyway, on this summer morning while Millie was gone, I went out to sit in the swing. I was out there enjoying the dew sparkling on the cotton plants, listening to the birds, and I remember I was barefoot. I was wearing a little sundress. Well, something, I don't know what, made me look over into that tree hollow."

Carol leaned forward. Her aunt's face looked ashen.

"Oh, honey, you can't imagine what was there! It was a big rattler."

"Oh," Carol shivered, "I would have died."

"Well, I did, I did. I froze. I died, I was stunned!"

"What about grandmother?"

"It seems like a dream, but just about that time, she came to the door and there I was frozen in the swing. I knew if I moved or anything that snake would strike."

"It was ready to strike?"

"As I remember, it wasn't rattling at first or I would have heard it. But when I saw it, it was coiled, its tongue flicking around, eyes bulging. I've had nightmares about it since. It was huge."

"Oh, Aunt Madden, I can't stand it. Go on."

"Well, there I was, frozen in the swing, that snake not more than two feet from me, and grandmother was by the screen door. She must have seen the horror on my face. I don't know how she knew it, but she said, and I'll never forget the way she said it, 'Madden, don't move.' "

"I was petrified. I didn't dare move my toes. I just sat there. The snake moved its head back and forth, rattled a time or two, I guess, I can't even say, then slithered down in the opposite direction. I can still see it. I can even see grandmother coming down the front steps of the farmhouse with a hoe. Papa was coming around the side of the house with a shotgun, I think. Grandmother's face was real hard looking, and she came toward me as quiet as an Indian. The rattler started slithering off toward the field, but it stopped and turned. Grandmother lifted that hoe and came down as hard as she could on that rattler. Papa stood by the corner of the house and fired. Grandmother cut off the rattler's head, and papa fired again. I'll never forget the way that snake wriggled! I was still frozen there in the swing, and grandmother started crying. Papa took her in his arms and she cried for almost an hour. They hugged me, and later I watched papa bury the snake. I knew they loved me."

"The other snake?"

"Oh, yes, the other snake. They watched for it and found it in the field nearby the next day. Papa killed it."

"After that?"

"No other snakes. We never saw any around there again, but things were never the same. When Millie and I went out to the tree or the swing, we'd always check the base of that cedar before we'd get close. And I always felt squeamish about sitting there. Uneasy, you know. But Millie and I never felt unloved again."

"Oh, wow!" Carol shivered. "And to think that's a real true story!"

"Millie said she would have died right then and there.

148

Well, I thought I was gone. It seemed unreal, like an awful dream. I didn't think there was a way out."

"And the charm?"

"That charm papa gave me years later. It was a tiny little hoe. He said it would remind me I was loved, very loved. I wore that charm for years and when grandmother died, I took it off. I don't know why. I was immature, maybe. I just never wore it again."

"Aunt Madden, I want to give it back to you."

"Of course not. I gave it to you. It's not valuable as a piece of jewelry, just sentimental."

"That's why I want you to have it. Please wear it for a while."

"Oh, my, honey. That doesn't make sense. This old world keeps turning around and people grow old and die and younger people take their place. It's the way things are supposed to be."

"Please wear it for me, Aunt Madden. You may not understand, but I need you to have it for a little while. I can have it back again, sometime."

"I can't, Carol. I can't. You're trying to turn things backward. Time goes forward—like the saying that a person can't control the length of his life, but he can have something to say about its width and depth."

"Aunt Madden, I don't know how to say this, but you've got to get well."

"You're fifteen years old, Carol. In the old days, you'd be a pioneer woman, maybe with a family already. Just because you live in these modern days, don't forget life is still tough. But life is better, more exciting, more opportunities, more miracles in science and research. It's a pretty fantastic time to be living."

"Aunt Madden, I'll never forget you. You can move to

Florida if you want to, but you'll always be close. If something happens to you, I'll—I'll—I . . . ."

"You can plant a cedar for me somewhere," Aunt Madden said and she laughed. "Don't worry. Things look good for me. Wear that charm sometimes and remember you belong to a good, strong family."

"In the land of the free and the brave, huh?"

"That's right," Aunt Madden continued. "With a YMCA where you can swim."

They laughed.

"With all this water everywhere, I still have to go to the Y to swim. Did I tell you? I'm going to call Mary Tree and ask her to go swimming this weekend."

"Good, good. Now tell me about school."

"Eldon's article about me came out today."

"Let me see it."

Carol showed her the paper. She watched while her aunt read.

"You know something, Carol, this is good. Really good."

"It was exciting, but just a coincidence."

"That's all right, Carol. That's life for you anyway. Nothing you can count on. The river always flows, never stops."

"We're just ripples in the stream, huh?"

"Yes," her aunt said, "but it's the ripples that catch the sunlight that make the river gleam."